CHOCO

Jack Callahan was born to fly...from the first time he felt the wind lift him above the dirt strip of a Wyoming ranch to later global contract flights, the cavalier pilot interpreted life through air currents and instruments. That was, until the afternoon his eye caught an art brochure in a Chicago airport...and Gage Bayswater McClendon walked out of his memory bank and ignited a powerful cerebral fire. He contacted the Metropolitan Gallery, cross-examined a receptionist and filed a flight plan.

Gage McClendon was sitting in a little cafe on the bank of the Mississippi River when the winsome flyer strolled to the table. His words, "you look just as I wanted you to look" were met with a powerful sensory surge... 'how often does the past come back looking like the past, handsome as hell'. The former USO worker and the veteran Vietnam pilot are spun into a whirlwind of intrigue that builds from the boil of a Chocolate Dancing weekend to an intense love story that unfolds from Chicago to Singapore.

Why did Al-Qaeda operatives fear the former Air Force major enough to put out a contract on him?

How would the challenges thrown at Callahan by Madame Nyugen factor into his relationship with Gage McClendon...and what of the tri-level steps of the mysterious keys...and the ultimate challenge of the golden rose?

Watch as the magic redoubles when a kraft paper wrapped painting becomes a principal player in this cabal of international intrigue.

Perhaps, the story of Jack Callahan and Gage McClendon is, indeed, 'the last great love story'.

CHOCOLATE DANCING
Copyright 2001 by Evelyn Boardman.
All rights reserved.
Tx u 747-531
ISBN 0-9753182-0-9

No part of this book may be reproduced, stored in a retrieval system, or transmitted by any means, electronic, mechanical, photocopying, recording, or otherwise, without written permission from the author.

Cover designed by
Don Greenwood

'to Dan, who could be Jack Callahan'

ABOUT THE AUTHOR

Evelyn Boardman lives in Cape Girardeau, Missouri where she serves on the city council and is an active advocate for social and political issues.

'the last great love story'

CHOCOLATE DANCING
EVELYN BOARDMAN

1

"It's a wonderful life!"

"You bet it is," Gage laughed, tugging at her briefcase. Nelson was a guru of cinematic trivia and he greeted her every morning with a pertinent movie title. He paced her steps and with uncanny timing swung open the oversized Gallery doors. The garrulous doorman was the first contact with Metropolitan Gallery every morning as well as the last echo of goodbye in the evening.

"They're all here, Ms Mac. Even Mr. Powell…he sure doesn't look like a man who was knockin' at heaven's gate a couple of months ago."

"Thanks, Nels," she barely answered. She was wondering what could bring Robert Powell, art patron extraordinaire, out so soon after a major heart attack. As the elevator doors opened, she took a last minute glance in the polished brass to make sure she didn't have cappuccino bubbles on her lapels.

Gage was Special Exhibits Director of one of Chicago's most prestigious Galleries. Her recent exhibits had been auspicious enough to raise the bar of Gallery standards to a level that could be difficult to sustain, but she intended to foster this status both for the Gallery and for herself. She'd developed considerable name recognition in the field of exhibit promotion. It was recognition that came in part because she was proficient at her job and in part because she'd been married to 'Mac' McClendon, an icon of Midwestern contemporary art. It was a show of his powerful abstracts that she had been working on for the past five months.

The Board Room door was open and the voices of the thirteen Directors sounded like a cassette tape in rewind. They were good people and they'd been more than fair with her when Mac died. She was given a month off to reorganize her life and work through the legalities of the estate. As Robert Powell took a seat at the head of the massive table, the other Directors followed. The Board meetings always resonated around his cohesive abilities.

"Gage, we wanted to get together to acknowledge our support in this exhibit. It seems to be coming together so smoothly, yet we know it's got to be difficult for you wearing two hats, so to speak," Mr. Powell's voice was thin and fragile as he framed his words.

Gage relaxed at hearing the purpose of this meeting and let her eyes sweep across their faces as she thanked them. Even so, she could feel waves of the deep seated widow blues washing up in her throat. She was aware of Mac's status in American contemporary art, but was very sensitive to the actual baring of his heart and soul in a way that would have suited him. He was very much his own person and her close involvement with him caused her a lot of concern as to whether she could be objective enough with this exhibit.

"He belongs to more than just his intimates," prompted Jeep Larkin, the only artist on the Board. "Gage, it'll be a grand tribute to Mac."

"Thanks, Jeep," she replied modestly.

"And quite bluntly, dear," murmured Lake Shore's Mrs. Addison Peavey Hunter, " the J.P. McClendon exhibit could help push us to a further level of achievement."

With a bit of a quiver to her voice, Gage reiterated a synopsis of the show.... why she'd chosen certain works, a little history of some of the paintings and finally the acknowledgment that not only did she owe it to the Board, but she also owed it to Mac to excel with this exhibit.

"There's one other point that I'd like to run by you," she continued. "I'd like to get another facet of Mac's work into the exhibit. I know it's late, but there are some wonderful oils down in his studio, wistful, bucolic abstracts. At first I didn't think we'd have space for them. But now that we're hanging, we have the room and I think they're right for the exhibit. I'd like to go to Missouri tomorrow to bring back a few of those pieces unless anyone has an objection." They agreed to her request, even old George Carlyle who always wanted to table everything until the next meeting. As diverse as these Directors were, they were overwhelmingly supportive of her and Gage felt extremely fortunate to work for them.

It was a given that as soon as the Board Meetings were over, Gage would pick up the phone and call Frank. He was her best friend, and at times they presented a scenario reminiscent of a couple of gossipy old maids.

"Can you meet me in thirty minutes at Anzio's?"

"Can do," Frank said wondering what was up. They'd had coffee together this morning as they did almost every morning and Gage hadn't mentioned anything that might call for a second hook up today.

A good looking guy with finely chiseled features, Frank Beccaccio vowed that he would never again be a licensed participant in a long term legal sentencing, otherwise known as marriage. He had a life of his own that included numerous beautiful women, but he and Gage had a special friendship that worked well for both of them. They could always count on each other and it made for a very strong alliance. Sometimes comical, other times serious, their relationship could be a sister- brother or a husband- wife or even a counselor- client dialogue that would wind through countless cups of coffee or one too many Bud Lights or even… depending on circumstances, maybe a bottle of a venerable chateau Sauternes.

Frank pulled his mirrored bronze Range Rover into Anzio's parking lot just as Gage crossed the street from the Metropolitan. He hopped out, stuffed a piece of Ghirardelli's dark chocolate in her hand and they chatted nonstop across the parking lot and through the single file coffee lines.

"The exhibit is almost ready," she beamed as she waited on caramel steamed milk. Frank was technically a photo journalist, but he was the official photographer for every Gallery exhibit that Gage had put together over the last five years. And during the last two years, he had become both her best friend and an accurate barometer of her equanimity.

"Great," he responded while rifling through the packets for the natural sugar crystals.

"Do you think it's possible that I haven't been objective enough on this one?"

"You're a consummate professional," Frank answered with a surgical clip to his voice. Gage relaxed and took a slow sip of the aromatic drink. One thing about Frank… he lived up to his name. He was opinionated and he was frank, and he didn't always say what she wanted to hear. On the other hand, there were times when she had to be more candid with him than she liked. When he was going through his divorce, she had to be a real bitch to get his focus beyond himself.

They had yet another bond that played out in their interactions. He was a military photographer for the Army during his hitch in Vietnam. Gage was a civilian employee with USO Special Services at Tan Su Nhut Air Base in Saigon setting up Rest and Recuperation breaks for the G.I.'s. Although their paths never crossed, Vietnam was always a common denominator. But it was rare that would Frank ever open up to the horrors drawn into his camera lens. Even so, at times he wore a sleeveless jacket, which with a little latitude of imagination resembled a flak jacket. Never mind that Beccacio's style was far too discriminating for an ordinary flak jacket. His was some pricey label's offering of a designer flak jacket. In all fairness, he did carry little canisters of film in the ammo-like pouches.

In the midst of a conversation that rambled from art to Spanish burnt sugar flan, Frank got to his feet. "I've got to get crackin'. I'm shooting a leggy blonde welcoming the whole world to the 'Taste of Chicago'." Gage smiled. Frank always got involved with his clientele. He walked with her to the Gallery parking lot and she went home to Poncho Sanchez, her over sensitive, overweight calico cat.

2

Morning sunlight strayed across the East windows of the apartment and highlighted the old gal's hair in the large oil painting 'Glory Between Scenes'. Who was the bold faced woman, worn and theatrical? Odd that she had never heard Mac explain the painting, maybe, even more odd that she'd never asked.

Gage suddenly remembered that she'd forgotten to tell Frank the very thing that she intended to tell him at Anzio's yesterday, that she was going to Missouri. She tried his cell phone. It was never hard to track him down. He always answered even if he was in the dark room in the middle of the developing process.

"Frank, I'm going down to Mac's studio this morning and bring back a couple more canvasses. I'll stay Thursday, Friday, and Saturday and be back Sunday afternoon. Would you please feed Pancho for me?" She didn't mind asking him. Last week she fed and pampered Noir, his big black Labrador when he went to his squadron reunion. "I'll leave the keys with the Giovanni's next door."

"Hold it, just hold on a minute. I'm right in the middle of a cup of Jamaica Blue Mountain and it calls for nice and easy." That was Frank alright…gadgets, girls, clothes, and coffees. It was his love affair with coffee that set him apart from most guys. He knew the name of every mountain in the world that had coffee beans on its slopes and he had a penchant for sixty dollar a pound coffees. "Want a cup for the road? I ordered it on the internet…from a wonderful high plateau roast station and I guarantee that it's a cup to die for…sweet and…oh, so delicious."

"You talking about coffee or 'leggy' Chicago?"

"Smart ass," he shot back.

Too bad that she didn't have time right now. When Frank was on a coffee high he talked. And it was only then that he would open up just a little window on Viet Nam. Gage found his reminiscences fascinating and knew they provided a certain catharsis for the old soldier in him. But right now, she thought of the words of Robert Frost…she had miles to go.

"I can't this time, Frank. It's seven hours down and I want to get on the road so I can miss rush hour traffic in St. Louis."

"Is it worse than Chicago's?"

Gage thought carefully before answering. "You know I think Chicago is more polite. I'm talking about drivers. St. Louis drivers seem to be always under the influence of road rage."

"Be careful, and don't worry about your kitty. And...hey, I'll miss you."

"Yeah you will, like you missed me last night."

"Come on, I was working. Gotta make a living."

"Sure, ...see you in a few days," she giggled and then dialed the Gallery.

Greta told her that she'd only had one call and that she told him to check back next week. She added, "He asked if your husband was originally from a Missouri town with Cape as part of the name. I hope I spelled Girardeau right for him. He said it was a nice name and I told him that you said that it was a very nice town and as a matter of fact that's where you'd gone to bring back some paintings for the upcoming exhibit."

"Okay, I'm off." And she headed her sporty Lexus toward I-55 South.

3

Selling his airplane was akin to selling his soul, but Jack Callahan was doing contract flying for Global Relief and didn't get back to the states often enough to justify having the beautiful Baron. He had mentioned rather casually earlier in the summer that he was thinking about selling the turbocharged Beechcraft. On the 4th of July, a friend who leased a hangar at Midway Airport had emailed him that a pizza group was looking for a medium sized twin engine plane for company use and they didn't want to get up into the Citation or King Air prices so they might be interested in buying his aircraft. He was due a flight physical in Atlanta anyway, so he worked Chicago into the trip.

When he bought the Baron, it was with the intention of flying it internationally. He'd been in the air most of his life. From the first dirt strip that he lifted off from in Wyoming as a sixteen year old greenhorn, to the temporary runways of Cam Ranh Bay to now... delivering essentials to places that you don't go to on vacation, Jack couldn't imagine life without gauges and instruments and maps. The Baron was the investment that others make in a home... like California real estate, he mused. He flew it transocean a few times and then like every other pilot, he got the "wants". He wanted to fly up over the amateurs and just under the jet traffic which would have meant a 58P and another hundred and fifty grand, and unless you plan on making your living with the plane, that didn't make a whole lot of sense. All dreaming aside, his matterhorn white, Baron 58TC with its burgundy and gray stripes was a pleasant, although expensive indulgence.

He walked to a pilots' rest area near the hangar to grab a cup of coffee and wait for the pizza people. Syrupy strong coffee was the only legal antidote for the long hours of contract flying. But a six figure contract was a damned good get well quick cure. He slung his long, lean body over a chrome bar stool and poured himself a powerful smelling cup.

A couple of airline pilots were talking about getting close to mandatory retirement age. They were obsessing over passing their next physical.

Jack hadn't thought much about it. He was going to Atlanta for his own physical Friday. He was still trim and agile. He worked out and ate as right as he could in countries where some of the food sources looked completely unfamiliar. When he'd listened long enough to what began to sound like juvenile whining from the two captains, he moved over to an easy chair near the window and picked up a 'Coming To Chicago' booklet. Leafing through the events, he stopped. He closed his eyes for a second and then looked again. "Christ!" he blurted out and sat up straight. He followed up with "Je......sus."

"You havin' a religious crisis over there?" one of the pilots asked facetiously.

"Sorry, something just caught my eye. Say, where's a phone with an outside line?"

"Back in the bunk area."

"Are you guys going to be here for a few more minutes. I'm waiting on some people who are coming to look at my Beechcraft and I've got to make a phone call."

"Gonna do confession over a phone," they jostled. " Sure go ahead, we'll be here until sky time." Jack started through to the bunk area when he saw what looked like a battalion of black suits walking around outside. It looked like they'd brought their entire pizza company.

"Oops, I'll use the phone later," he said as he hurried past the jokers.

"Can we call her for you?"

Pilots were notoriously corny. Jack knew he'd made some of the same silly comments and he winced at the thought. The black suits waited patiently. They brought their own pilot and he seemed to be quite familiar with Barons, both their charm and their idiosyncrasies. So he gave a brief run through and stepped back to let them give full attention to the aircraft. Then he took the pilot and a couple of the company execs up for a drive and showed off a bit for them. At the risk of sounding like a pimp for his lady, he toned down his sales pitch. Back on the ground, he gave them the manuals and logs and left them alone for awhile.

He walked back to the rest area, made his telephone call, then chatted a few minutes with the two pilots. Out of the corner of his eye, he could see that the pizza caucus was about to disband so he strolled out to listen to the price haggling or financing contingencies, one or the other, or both ... no doubt the next step. But they simply said that they'd let him know something within a week. Oh well, he thought, it really didn't matter right now anyway. He needed to gas up. He was taking the Baron for a little trip this afternoon.

4

Traffic always moved fairly well on I-55 through Illinois. However, Missouri had a higher speed limit so she looked forward to the Welcome to the Show Me State signs. Enya's new Cd and a couple of old Cat Stevens discs got her to Bloomington. At that point Gage turned on talk radio and in a captive situation succumbed to being a part of the groupie listeners to a right wing talk show host. It was a man whose mouth didn't seem to be connected to a discernible mind. His inflammatory rhetoric made her all the more proud that she'd been labeled a flaming liberal. It was the first time that she could ever remember truly wanting to smash a radio. After the doubletalk prattlings there was enough adrenaline pumping to cruise all the way through St. Louis and into Cape Girardeau without any caffeine or any hint of tiredness.

Gage pulled the car up to the studio and sat for a few minutes looking through the big windows. She could see canvasses lined up around the walls, paintings stacked on the long oak table, and pots and pots of brushes silhouetted against the sun. She should have done something earlier with the studio, either rented it or even sold it, but she just didn't have an inkling of what to do with the art. It was never very convenient that the studio was so far from Chicago. But Mac loved both the city and the area where he grew up. So he became the quintessential commuter. Fifteen minutes was all it took for the first visitor to knock on the rustic ochre door. Although the door was standing open to let in a little fresh air, Santa Fe was always rather formal in his mannerisms. "Santa Fe, come on in. How the hell have you been?" She was sincerely thrilled to see him. He, too, was an artist and had been Mac's best friend. Her husband always thought that Santa Fe was the better artist, and that it was only Mac's connections in Chicago that allowed him to achieve a celebrity status.

She looked around for a bottle of wine to offer a drink, but remembered that he was no longer a drinker. He hadn't given up cigarettes though. If you squinted, you could almost see the smoke layered on his leathery skin. There was something about Santa Fe that you just had to love. He rambled around a story until you might just end up back at the beginning of a twenty minute conversation without having ever known where you went or why.

"Didn't know you were coming or I'd have bought you a little vino caveat emptor," he said with a W.C. Fields flair. "I hope you don't mind that I've been making some stretchers and using the miter box . I'm sure you're aware, I have impeccadilo credentials in Clean Up 101."

"I'm glad you feel comfortable here," Gage offered. Worrying about Santa Fe cleaning anything up would be about the most wasted worry in the world. If anything, he was OCD. His obsessive compulsiveness was certainly apparent in his loft studio. Each tube of paint was perfectly placed side by side, even squeezed at the same place in the tube. Nothing was random in his world except his communication skills, all you had to do was throw out a subject and he would take it to China and back.

She couldn't resist, "What's new, Santa Fe?"

" I think I went back to New Mexico since you were down here last. My car broke down before I got to Oklahoma and Margie had a clinic to do to in St. Louis so we ended up doing the touristy things. It was probably a good thing that the doodle bug didn't make it all the way because those paintings were still on the table at home. You can have one if you'd like."

She rested her case. He hadn't let her down. Who really cared what he talked about anyway? Those roller coaster conversations were part of what everyone loved about him. Gage broke into his story, "I've come to take back some paintings for Mac's show and I need your artistic insight and expertise. And yes, I would love to have one of your pieces."

She stopped short for a second and realized that she should try to get Santa Fe a show in Chicago. He had some great credentials. He was formerly a University Art instructor and at one time had taught in the same Texas public school system as Georgia O'Keefe.

"You know," Gage framed the words slowly as not to get his hopes too high, "I would like to have a portfolio of your work to take to my Board. Could you get something together for me in the next few months?" He had a most unique and individualistic style. His acrylics were clear and clean and his subject matter was imagination run amuck. The art world loves characters and with Santa Fe, they would be getting a hundred and fifty percent character. He came out of the decadent years of drugs and alcohol a little more decadent than most of his peers. He looked healthy enough now with his dark tan and white beard and he probably weighed about the same as he did in the eighth grade. But the man was one savvy expert in the field of art.

It was a definite possibility that if she could just get him to Chicago, he could mesmerize the Board. She could see them now in wide eyed amazement at the dialogue fostered by this slight built artist talking in combination of similes, parables, and playful adjectives.

They wandered around the studio unstacking and sorting the artwork and after a couple of hours Santa Fe began to look either tired or bored, Gage couldn't tell which. She suggested that they call it quits for the evening.

"How about a light supper down at Grant's Place tonight? It's pay back time for the generous use of the studio," Santa Fe suggested." Later on, there's a local blues band playing."

Supposedly, General Grant had been a guest of this old establishment during the Civil War, hence the name. It could have been true. The old brick building set on the bank at the edge of the Mississippi River, but whether or not General Grant ever set foot inside, it made a good story. Gage looked forward to the evening. The studio had a build up of August heat, and a glance in an old mirror near the door showed a perspiration soaked body that needed to shower before leaving the premises. She unlocked the little apartment that had literally grown on the back of the studio one room at a time....first a bathroom, then a bedroom and finally a pullman kitchen. It wasn't much, but there was always a real 'down home' ambience about the place.

5

What local color! No wonder Mac loved it here. As always, the big round table was circled with familiar faces and each one had to have a hug…. true Midwestern hospitality. The old downtown had long been a gathering place for the arty as well as the quirky. Greenwood was there, so Gage knew that there would be some good harmonica. They talked loud and laughed hard and downed great platters of catfish and hushpuppies. She supposed that no where else in the world except along this great river did people actually eat catfish. It wasn't easy to answer all their questions and eat at the same time, so she finally gave up on social graces and talked with her mouth mushed full. "You guys, just don't know how heart warming it is to see you again." Her words brought more hugs, this time a tad more slippery and greasy in the clinches. But as 'country' as this scene might look to an outsider, this laid back group was as educated and as talented as any group you could put together in Chicago.

"Aw, we're just plain ole 'swamp east' Missouri." This local jargon came from a playwright, a gal who was also an instructor at Southeast Missouri State University.

Gage was emphatic, "Seriously, look around here. There are three artists, an engraver, a photographer, two novelists, and a playwright".

"Excuse me," Cindy, the hostess interrupted their chatter. "Ms. McClendon, there's a man at the bar who is asking how to find a Gage, I think he said…Bayswater. You're the only Gage I know," she said half apologetically.

Gage didn't connect with her maiden name for a second, but she began a ninety degree turn in the direction of Cindy's nod. Before her eyes made contact with the bar, she was greeted with, "Gage Bayswater…Jack Callahan."

She stood up, drew in a deep breath, then took another breath even deeper and in slow motion the words scrolled out her mouth, "Major JC Callahan… oh… my… god!" How often does the past come back looking like the past, handsome as hell. She stumbled around in a feeble attempt at introductions while trying to figure out what on earth he was doing here and why.

"I was in the neighborhood," was his comment.

It was as though her brain was in a 'stun' mode, although she did think to ask him if he would like to join her at a small table near the wall.

"You look very much like I remember...and just the way what I wanted you to look," he said softly. He touched her chin and tilted it to the light. "Perfect!"

"Well, so do you... I can't believe it is really... you. It was thirty years ago that she worked in the USO Recreation Center in Vietnam. She could still see the undaunted young pilot in this mellow and attractive man. The years had been more than kind to him. Her mind kept processing the same word over and over. "Damn!"

The waitress took up the slack in an awkward pause, "Can I get you drinks?"

Turning to Gage, Jack smiled, "Do you remember the Galliano drink, Golden Cadillac?"

"You remember that? We thought we were pretty cosmopolitan, didn't we? But I don't think you could find a bartender anywhere today who'd know how to concoct one."

"I don't want one. I don't think I could handle it now," he laughed. "Just wondered if you remembered it." He ordered Glenlivet neat.

Remembering the soft licorice taste, Gage ordered Sambucca. She waited while the waitress shouted their orders to the bartender and then confronted this virtual reality of a past era sitting across from her with, "How and why?"

"To the 'how'... how did I find you? I flew into Chicago this morning to meet with prospective buyers for my airplane. While waiting for them, I picked up a City Guide that mentioned an upcoming art exhibit of McClendon works put together by the gallery's Special Exhibits Director who was also the artist's widow, Gage McClendon. Now, I'm thinking back to Vietnam and an attractive young woman working so hard to help keep a bunch of horny bastards happy by scheduling R & R's out of the country for them. Guess what, same unusual name. I remembered that she told me that she was engaged to an artist from Cape Girardeau, Missouri. I thought she was making the name up since it was unlikely that a city in the middle of the country would have a name with Cape in it. To make a long story short, this morning I called the Gallery, questioned the receptionist and filed a flight plan. As to 'why', I don't know... but why not?"

"How's your wife?"

"Which one? Marney got tired of competing with the Air Force and she left me for a dentist who eventually fell in love with his hygienist. Then ten years ago I was ferrying cropdusters to Central America and I married a Panamanian beauty. Later, we found out that it wasn't a legal marriage and beauty was superficial. I eventually drifted away."

Gage swirled her crystal clear drink and watched the muddy rivers of the Mekong Delta surface to the mellow harmonica strains of "When I Lost You Baby, I Almost Lost My Mind".

"But you were married."

" My mistake." He smiled and said nothing for a long minute and let the melancholy music pull him to where he didn't go very often. "Hey, I didn't find you to put us both in a blue funk. Tell me about yourself? Obviously, you've been married once... to the artist, right?"

"Right."

"And obviously, there is an inland Cape... and obviously, you never knew that I purposely used every excuse that I could think up to get back up to Special Services as often as possible."

"I was twenty-six years old and you were 'a dragon man', a sacred cow for pete's sake... the next to God, Major Jack Callahan," she laughed.

She helped him schedule a trip to Hong Kong once and he brought her back a jewel faced watch. He was the only one of the guys she ever really spent any time with. He seemed different than the others and, yes, she was aware of the chemistry between them. They shared hours of talking and dancing at the USO whenever he was in from the Bien Thuy wilderness. Jack was from the Fourth Corps, Air Commandoes, flying AC-47 Spookies. It was a fact that the Spooky crews had one of the most dangerous jobs in Vietnam. They were flying a plane that would come in slow and low and fire Gatling guns from the side door spewing 6,000 rounds of ammo per minute, so fast that it looked like fire coming out of a dragon's mouth. Even the enemy, who was superstitious by nature, didn't like to upset the dangerous 'dragons'. Puff the Magic Dragon was a popular song in the states about then and the name carried over to the AC-47's.

"You were right, Ms. Bayswater McClendon, the timing was wrong then. You're just staring at your Sambucca. Would you like a different drink?"

"No," she sighed. "I was thinking about the first time I saw you. You'd just come up from the Mekong River after 'taking out' Viet Cong sampans. You looked like you belonged to any other country's air force but ours. You were wrinkled, rumpled, grubby and greasy... and so sweaty! But you know, I remember thinking that you smelled sexy."

"Thanks, but Viet Nam was definitely synonymous with your adjectives and clean up facilities were few and far between."

"And you'd been sent up to Tan Son Nhut to pick up a Colonel and take him back to Bien Thuy and I recall that he insisted you guys take a shower before he went back with you."

Jack thought for a second and laughed, "Guess he didn't think I smelled sexy." He ordered another scotch and listened as strains of Streets of Laredo wailed above the chatter of the bar. "Do you want to know what I remember about that day?" And without giving her a chance to answer he reached over and picked up her left hand and touched the wedding band. "The first thing I did back then was to look and see if you were wearing a wedding ring... and you were! So I almost didn't say anything to you, but I happened to see what appeared to be a rather guilty look on your face when you saw me look at your hand."

Gage responded, "We were told that wearing wedding rings might be a good idea. I never thought much about it until you put me on the spot. Then I finally had to admit to just being engaged."

"You're still wearing a wedding ring. Is it still to keep the troops away?"

"No... well, yes... there's a certain security factor in it." She didn't pull her hand away even though she knew he could feel her cool fingers becoming warm and moist. They talked on and on without ever changing the position of the clasped hands. It was as if they moved them then there might not be a reason to bring them back together. The evening went on until Gage realized that her friends had gone and the bar had started a clean up of clinking glasses. "Major, would you like to see the riverfront? Come on, let's go for a walk"

"Sounds good, let's go... but I am going to have to leave soon. My plane is out at your airport and I've got a two day flight physical ahead of me in Atlanta. The group that I met with in Chicago this morning promised to let me know by Friday if they're going to buy my plane. If all works out I'll be back this way Saturday. Are you going to be around here?" It didn't really matter where she'd be, he could find her anywhere now. "And would you like to do something?" He was still holding her hand as they walked along the banks of the Mississippi, two long ago friends, not really knowing enough about each other and yet afraid of losing the moment.

"I'll be finishing up here Saturday, so... yes, I'd like that."

"Give me a phone number."

Gage wrote down her cell phone number and they started back up the river bank. He walked back to the studio with her and they stood awkwardly and quietly talking. He could see her legs outlined in her skirt through the streetlight. The heavy humidity pulled the thin blouse close to her chest revealing a moistened outline of supple nipples. He tried to keep his focus on leaving.

"Callahan, she called out as he started back to his rental car, "I forgot to ask you where and what kind of flying you're doing now." She assumed he was still flying full time, pilots don't quit until they can't pass a physical or they paste away.

"Indonesia... contract flying, relief supplies," he yelled, not looking back... afraid that the street light might pull him back.

She stood silhouetted without moving, listening to crickets in the night heat and watching him walk away in the same upbeat stride that she'd seen time and time again years ago in a crazy war in a strange little country on the other side of the world.

6

The streets of Atlanta were as congested as those in Jakarta and he was a quart low on patience when it came to city traffic. Running short on time, he called for a courier, a traffic shortcut expert, who picked him up and maneuvered the ramps and exits with the skill of board game strategy. It was somewhere around 04:00 when he landed so he slept in the plane and cleaned up in the pilots locker rooms. He'd check into the hotel after he got started on the tests.

As always with guys, everyone was ' old buddy' with back slaps and handshakes. It had a lot to do with breaking the tension. It was always in the back of your mind that your couldn't keep perfect health forever. A 'grounded' notice might as well be accompanied by an obituary notice. They all worried, even the hot shot 'top gun' at the head of the line. One blood test out of sync or an eye chart not quite sharp enough, they were valid concerns. They coughed together, pee'd together, did blood work together, and later drank together if everything went well.

The over 55's got a hell of a work out on the tread mills. Callahan thought he was in good shape, but the doc's kept raising the degree of incline just to see how close they could come to killing them.

In the two days of work-ups, work-outs and quizzing from Psychology 101, every last one of the guys in his group were certified physically fit to celebrate. They partied like old friends, long and loud, venting all the anxiety of some damn test coming along to trip them up. Jack partied partly to appease the gods of celebration and partly because he'd had a call from the pizza people. They wanted to buy his Beechcraft and they came close enough in price. They asked that one instrument be re-calibrated and that could be done in St. Louis. The sale of the plane was part of his unsettled state of mind, but he knew that a greater part of it had to be her. He couldn't wait to get back to the Midwest.

"Got to move on, guys," he said after a few hours of bar hopping.

"Cherchez la femme," 'top gun' called out.

"Got some paperwork," Jack answered. He really did want to get the papers in order for the sale and he'd intended to call Gage tonight rather than tomorrow. But that idea was nixed posthaste when he glanced at his watch and realized the lateness of the night.

Meanwhile, Gage worked two full days in the studio with only a small oscillating fan between her and the ninety-two degrees of heat and humidity typical of August in the Midwest. Santa Fe came to her rescue a couple of times with cold bottled water. He spent a lot of time talking art history and that helped pass time. Funny, but when he was in his field of expertise you didn't need a roadmap to follow him. He was brilliant! He even taught her a little about mediums and techniques. Finally, she had to ask because he hadn't mentioned anything, and she was curious at his perception of Wednesday night, "Santa Fe, what do you think of my friend?"

"Well, I guess it was H.L. Mencken who said, 'An idealist is one who, on noticing that a rose smells better than a cabbage, concludes that it will also make better soup'."

"Ohhhhkay." She forgot for a moment that she'd asked a question from outside the fine arts part of the brain. The guy was either so damn intelligent that you couldn't connect with him or so mucked up that you needn't try. Then, as if the question was too invasive, he announced that it was time for him to retreat to his loft.

A glance at her watch reminded her that the day was winding down and she hadn't talked to Frank. She dialed and waited for the familiar, 'yea'. He figured that if you had his cell phone number, you were a friend and didn't need a further greeting.

"Yea."

"Hello, I sure could use a cup of coffee."

"Where are you?" He looked down at the phone in his hand as if he expected her to appear from inside.

"I'm in the studio, almost finished."

"Well, if you're gonna be back by tomorrow evening, I've got two tickets to the Jazz Expo and I won't try to pick up a chick…"

"Frank, listen to me." Sometimes you had to stop him cold to get his attention and she was eager to tell him about tomorrow. It wasn't like she'd never been out, she had dinner occasionally with male acquaintances. But she usually ran it by Frank first. No reason, just somehow it had gotten to be a habit. But explaining this scenario to him, she wasn't even sure she could explain it to herself. "Uh, I probably won't be back in time, but thanks, go ahead and do your 'pick up a chick' thing. I know this sounds freakish for me, but there's someone that I knew a long time ago…"

"Excuse me," he butted in "but just how long ago are we talking about, five minutes or five hours or what? You've only been gone two days."

Gage cleared her throat, "Uh, well…thirty years ago."

"Holy shit, you're in small town America and you've breathed too much methane manure. Come on Gage, he's probably an opportunist who thinks you are a rich woman from the big city."

"Frank," she chuckled, " your Sicilian roots are showing." For many generations his family owned orange groves around Paterno, Sicily. Shortly before World War II broke out, his grandfather migrated to the Tuscan area of Italy sending Frank's father and mother, Benito and Nana, to live with relatives in Chicago. His wariness or downright suspicious nature was a gift of his Sicilian heritage. "I appreciate your concern, but I'm just fine, maybe I'm even better than fine. I'm just great. I'll call as soon as I get in. How's Pancho?"

"The cat's okay, but you...he's a gigolo, that's gotta be it."

"Cool it pal, I've got my head on straight and I'm a big girl." Interesting association between herself and Frank, there was a bit of protectiveness to a point of possessiveness on both sides. It was a friendship that ran right up to the edge of a relationship, but never quite crossed the line. It was emotional and deep rooted and it worked. "Make time for me when I get back Sunday afternoon, I have plenty to tell you."

"I've never heard you like this."

"I know. See you later." She hung up and looked up the phone number of a local real estate agent who had a side business of auctioneering. She had decided to list the property and let him auction the studio equipment. Arrangements were made to pack and ship the paintings back to Chicago, except for the few she was going to take back with her. Reluctantly, she and Santa Fe culled and destroyed those they knew Mac wouldn't want out on the market.

Tomorrow morning she could work out the details with the realtor. When she was driving down she thought that she'd like to hear rain on the old tin roof one more time and just as she finished the phone calls a harsh rain began to pummel the tin. She had to scurry to close the windows. Gage sat cross legged on the old window seat watching the rain and thinking. She thought a lot about tomorrow...... a whole lot about tomorrow.

7

He was out of bed and was shaving when the desk rang with his wake up call. There were a few errands to run before heading to the airport and by staying at the downtown Hyatt he could walk to a couple of good department stores. He thought his clothes were in better shape than they'd looked in the mirrored wall, so he put clothes on his list of errands.

It was eight o'clock, still too early to call Missouri, and the stores hadn't opened yet. So it looked like he'd have to partner up with a weight room again. It was always the weight rooms in hotels where he spent time before anything opened or after everything closed.

After hour or so of working out and a cooling down shower, he knew he must call her now and get it off his mind. He punched in the area code and then the numbers and the phone rang and rang, a long time, too long. What if she hadn't waited?

"Hello," a breathless but cheery hello.

"Hi, it's Jack."

Gage felt a tightening of her lower stomach muscles. "I recognize your voice. Excuse me, I was outside showing a realtor the property and had to run back inside."

"It's okay." He gave a long whistle under his breath. She had waited. " I'm heading your way about noon, but I've got to leave the Baron in St. Louis for some work. I think I'll rent a car and drive down, but it might be 4:30 before I get there."

"Major, I'm sure I'll be through here by early afternoon and I'll be going North anyway. Why don't we meet in Ste. Genevieve? It's just to the left of I-55 about halfway, a quaint little town, French background."

"Sounds good. Did you say Ste. Guinevere? Hey, by the way, 'Major' was a long time ago. It's just Jack."

"Yes, sir," she said mockingly. "And, it's Ste. Genevieve. There's a little brick restaurant in the center of the town that's been there forever, you can't miss it. Let's plan on 4:30. But if anything changes, would you mind calling me?"

"Nothing will change, I'll be there. Can I bring or do anything for you?"

Impulsively and without any hesitation Gage said, "Just touch me."

"My pleasure, over and out." The errands, the airport, St. Louis, and the blessed French lady town, he was tempted to skip the errands. He even thought for a moment about checking to see if Genevieve city had an airport. "Whoa, guy," he said to himself. "Slow down, over the years you've taken a lot of risks and are still walking and it wasn't by being irrational and impulsive."

She was thinking... new dress. Grabbing her purse, she breezed through the door and headed toward Main Street. The perplexed realtor was still waiting alongside the studio. She caught his image out of the corner of her eye and backtracked, "I guess we were about finished, weren't we?" He reached in his pocket and handed her his card. She'd already filled out the paperwork that he'd brought with him, so she thanked him and hurried along .

Two blocks away was a stylish women's store. It had a distinct old world look complete with frescoed ceiling. There was a knock-out dress in the window the other evening on the way to Grant's Place. " Mrs. McClendon," came a sweet southern drawl across the store. Max and her husband owned a group of ladies apparel shops around the Midwest. "How are you, dear?"

"Very well, thanks," Gage acknowledged without further elaboration. "Do you, by any chance have the red spaghetti strap dress in the window in a size eight, or close?" She waited while they meticulously checked the racks. Bingo, they had it and it was gorgeous. At the dressing room, she had to wade through the compliments of all the clerks in the store, an old and successful selling ploy. She didn't need their input, she knew it was perfect. Pulling weeds around the studio had given her tan just enough boost that she might not wear the bolero jacket that came with it.

She was glancing at her reflection in the window glass of the furniture store as she dashed by and almost ran into the proprietor, affectionately known as 'Mr. Downtown'. He said facetiously and with a big grin, "Big hurry, got a date?" And she remembered that he'd stopped by the table to say hello the other night at Grant's Place. "Hi, how are you?" she asked without answering his question.

The sun was beginning an afternoon slant as she ran the water for a bath. She had trouble keeping a focus. Bath, oh yes....bath, and nails retouched and steam from the bath to take out a faint wrinkle in the dress. It was as if, she was moving in slow motion and having to doubly concentrate on her tasks. What was it about this guy?

She'd been trying to think back to everything that she could remember about him. How the other officers called him by his initials, JC. And when they really wanted to get his attention, they called him Jackson Calhoun Callahan. Whether that was his name or what, no one ever said. He was considerate and kind and she recalled that he brought a certain calm to her war zone workplace. She stood at the edge of the bed for a moment wondering if she was having any kind of effect on him. He did look her up after all! Lifting the clingy red dress gently from the hanger, she pulled it slowly over her head and adjusted the straps. Three times she adjusted the straps.

8

Shopping was not a dominant Callahan gene. But he dodged the cars to a safe crossing at the busy intersection near the hotel because he'd already established in his mind that he needed a wardrobe update. The last time he'd been clothes shopping was a year ago in Malta. He'd bought then what he was looking for now, pale tan light weight khaki shirt and pants. His sister said he looked like a walking Banana Republic Store. He didn't know much about the store, but he sure as hell knew a lot about banana republics. He didn't find khaki, but he did find a couple of good fitting linen shirts, a dressy tan T-shirt, and a new pair of Levi's. It took longer than he wanted, but there was still plenty of time to take the underground back to the airport.

"Got my plane ready, Pete?" He'd called ahead to have it brought out and gassed up.

"Yep, big guy, she's lookin' good and ready to go."

"Thanks, buddy." He paid up, did a walk around and waited for the tower to move him out. Next stop Lambert Airport. Flying was the easy part, threading his way through the maze of interstate road repairs in St. Louis was not half as much fun. Still, he was on schedule. He tuned in an easy listening station. The only rental cars left on the lot were the luxury cars, Merc's and Jag's. He didn't much like Mercedes', so he'd taken the keys to a new Jaguar XKJ. It was a vehicle to soothe even the most beastly of souls. The smooth ride, easy listening, and anticipation of a beautiful summer evening made the straight line interstate roll by rapidly. Twenty miles to Ste. Genevieve on the big green road sign...he liked Guinevere better. He didn't have a clue who Genevieve was, but he did know that Guinevere, Lancelot, and King Arthur were part of some mystical medieval love triangle.

Gage put a Kris Kristofferson disc in the CD player and took the Silver Tongued Devil himself all the way to Ste. Gen. There was something about that voice, that street smart, whiskey throated sound that locked her attention and he was the one distraction that could keep her mind off 4:30 p.m. She didn't care that it wasn't current or that she heard it so many times, she even sang along occasionally.

There was plenty of parking around the little restaurant, it wasn't time for the dinner crowd. She sat with the engine running, couldn't cut Kristofferson off in the middle of a song, and checked to make sure she had her credit cards and that her cell phone was charged. In a matter of minutes, a handsome pilot tapped on the window and Gage unlocked the door. He opened it and swung into the seat beside her, "Every blasted mile I thought about you, girl. I crashed three times."

"What?" she said startled.

"Just kidding, god you're beautiful."

"You're pretty terrific looking yourself, former Major, now just Jack."

"Thanks. Let's close down this restaurant and have it all to ourselves," he sounded serious.

"We can't do that," Gage was defensive as they entered the building.

"I know, darling, but we can pretend."

She laughed. She hadn't been in the world of free spirits in such a long time that she'd forgotten there are those who do pretend and take risks and push boundaries.

Jack joked with the bartender, told him that they would be homesteading a forty square foot area for the evening and that no one was to cross the property line unless they were bringing food or drinks. The burly barkeeper with his deep, laughing voice became a willing player in this early evening pretense. Seemingly, sensing that it was more than just an ordinary evening for the 'homesteaders', his role evolved into perimeter guard as well. "No, you can't sit there folks," he'd bellow when anyone got near the couple, " those two have a fever and are in quarantine." He was funny and he was fun. Jack asked his name and he said it was Domino. He was quick to explain, " it's really Dominick, but around these parts, everybody calls me Domino."

"Well, Domino, it is then. Would you fix us a couple of sloshy frozen midwestern Margaritas?" Jack asked.

"Will do, if you'll tell me what the hell, a 'midwestern' margarita is?"

"Dunno, seems a lot of things take a different slant here in the Midwest...maybe, it's extra lime to keep down the scurvy out here on the prairie."

Domino slapped his towel on the bar and gave a 'thumbs up'. "Got it mate, extra lime, it is."

Gage listened intently as Jack brought this big burly man into an inner circle. Men and women really do go about things in vastly different ways.

"Excuse my manners," Jack turned back to Gage. He reached across the table and lifted both her hands and held them sandwiched between his palms. "Is 'touch me' still an option?"

At that moment the margaritas arrived and the waiter interrupted to announce that he'd brought a dish of extra limes. They drank a toast to Domino and Ste. Genevieve.

Gage never did answer his question, didn't think she needed to. She took a lime wedge, sprinkled a little salt and handed it to him. They talked and laughed and looked at each other at times like old lovers and other times like teenagers on a first date.

"Tell me more about your life, where you've been or traveled all these years, what exotic places you've flown into, what close calls you've had?" she plied.

"Every place I've been, every path I've taken. It was all about getting to this little Missouri sainte lady town to have an evening with a gal that I can't shake from my thoughts and can't bury in my memories. And, in case if you haven't noticed, I'm a pretty mellow guy right now."

"I noticed. And for what it's worth, mellow looks good on you. As a matter of fact, your outback demeanor is very becoming. Even your clothes have a sort of mellowness about them… and well, hell, you're a very sexy guy, JC."

"What a day, what a town, what a delight." He turned toward the bar. " Domino, we need menu's. You gonna stay with margaritas, Gage? I think I'll just have a shot of tequila… and salt."

"Order me a shot of tequila, too, and a shaker of salt. We've got to use up all these limes."

Domino brought the menus over but didn't lay them on the table. He spoke as if whispering a secret, "Grilled swordfish is fantastic. This isn't supposed to be the night for it, but the cook got a fresh shipment this morning. Try it, you'll like it, I guarantee."

"Sounds good to me," Gage said.

"Make it two. I haven't had grilled swordfish since I was in Portugal. Have you been there?"

"No, but it is on my 'to do' list", she replied.

"Well, let me tell you about that little country. The evenings are balmy and the stars are sparkling. The seafood is magnificent. If you want swordfish, it might take an hour or so to get it and with good reason, because it wouldn't be at all uncommon after you order to see a couple of fishermen lugging a fresh swordfish up a side terrace. You start the evening with a fantastic white wine and a classic fish soup. Come to think about it, the only thing missing from a perfect evening in Portugal was you. Want to go to Portugal? And if you'd like we could do a whole seafood circuit... Marseille, home of the world's best bouillabaisse with saffron and fennel, or the Greek Isles for beachside grilled sardines in olive oil and ouzo."

"Pilots and gastronomy, I guess it's a likely combination. Go for the gold. You're one free spirit, aren't you. No boundaries, no barriers."

"There are no boundaries, no barriers, luv...sometimes consequences, but no barriers or boundaries. Give me your wrist."

She stretched out her arm and he rubbed the inside of her wrist with lime and covered it with salt. He raised it in the air, licked the salt from her wrist and chased it with tequila. She felt effervescent. Maybe it was the drink, maybe it was just plain happiness. Whatever, it was fun.

"Can I?" She reached for his wrist and squeezed a little lime juice, tapped on salt and stroked the mixture with her fingertips.

"Be still, my heart. I'm under the power of an elixir mixer. I don't want to break this spell, but did you buy that ravishing red dress for tonight or is this what a gallery director normally wears when off duty?"

"Mr. Major Callahan," she leaned forward and in a very scintillating whisper replied, "you seem to have all the answers...you tell me."

"Whoops, saved by a swordfish," he grinned as the waiter reached over their arms to place the saltwater delicacy before them.

Gage caught the waiter's attention, "Would you please bring a bottle of Alsace riesling, maybe a Trimbach or Beyer."

"A what," said the young man.

"Sorry," she smiled, "any riesling will be fine."

"Ho, you've been holding back, haven't you... should have known, you were wine savvy, another facet of you as a class act. Headlines read..." Jack gestured as if reading a newspaper, "Gage McClendon , a vision of haute cuisine in red crepe. I hope I can make this evening worthy of the vision sitting across from me. I don't know whether it's because you take me back to a younger time or because you let me see that it's great to be where we are right now. Perhaps, it's the potency of the combination, but this is indeed the ultimate richness of life."

She knew what he was feeling, she was on the same crescendo. When her bottle of wine came to the table, they toasted the moment and indulged the sweet pleasures of food and drink and the glorious presence of one another.

"Meet me in Singapore," Jack couldn't help but think beyond this week.

"Affirmative," she said dreamily.

All the while the bartender held the perimeter around them, keeping a quiet surveillance over two people lost to their surrounds and caught in their own delightful enthusiasm. He watched them laugh and drink and eat without taking their eyes off of each other. He saw the lady take olives with her fingers and hold them out to the guy in khaki. He noticed that as their fingers touched, their eyes talked to each other. And he savored his bit part in the sequence.

9

The noisy sounds of evening began to unfold. A four piece band worked diligently at putting itself together. Gage began to wonder whether her friend had prearranged something with the gregarious bartender. Domino was taking on overtones of a housemother, moving the musicians a few feet back of an apparently familiar position and doing it with a kindness aimed at keeping everyone happy.

"You're going to like the music tonight," he announced gleefully. "They may not look like uptown guys, but their music is hot. Whatever you want they can play it. Their specialty is country and retro soft rock... but mostly country."

"Sounds super," Jack assured him and Gage lifted a fork speared with a crust of swordfish in approval. The preparation of the food was superb and the presentation was exquisite. The little town had lived up to its French heritage.

"Jack, how about a drink to the gods of good fortune? I couldn't feel anymore blessed than I do right at this moment."

"Hold on just a second." He gave a quirky little bar language hand signal to Domino that effected raised eyebrows and a big grin. The bar area of the restaurant had a full crowd by now, mostly regulars who seemed to be friends of the musicians.

"A round of drinks on this guy," Domino called out pointing a finger and working hurriedly without raising his head. "With a toast as soon as I can get the drinks," he added tilting his head toward Jack as if to make sure that he'd read the signals right. Those near by called out their thanks as the bartender began to load the drinks on a tray.

"Wow! Aviator friend, you're full of surprises," Gage murmured in a soft teasing undertone. "I believe you're really into this evening, you certainly know how to make a gal feel special."

"That's what I want to hear. We're in charge of the universe tonight, babe. Stand up." He pulled her to her feet and tapped on his glass.

Domino helped a little with a loud, "Shut up, you lugheads."

Jack looked at Gage and then at the bar crowd. "I've flown under, over, and through the skypaintings we call rainbows, ever coveting those gossamer beauties and always looking for that lucky end of the rainbow. Raise your glasses, please, to this fantastic lady. I've just found the end of the rainbow!"

There were cheers and applause and a din of good natured ribbing and a "Let's hear what the lady has to say."

"Okay," Gage volunteered. "I'd like to tell Skyking here that he is totally just as handsome now as when he used to wave at me through the window of his plane as he taxied down the airstrip at Tan Son Nhut."

She was immediately interrupted by a loud and boisterous, "You were Nam? Me too! Let's hear it for Viet Nam." And the whole bar erupted into three or four minutes of raucous whoops and hollers.

"Looks like you're the one who's set the tone for the evening," Jack quipped as the noise persisted. They'd wakened a sleeping ghost, roused some old warriors.

She smiled. Then with a rather puzzled expression said , "You sounded like an artist with your skypainting and gossamer reference. Are you?"

"Am I what, an artist? More painter than artist. I've always dabbled. When we were kids my folks used to take us camping up in Canada near Kicking Horse Pass and I always took my watercolors. Never painted anything much as it was. I always painted things as I thought they would look next season or in the case of a baby animal, the way it would look grown up. Strange little quirk, and it always drove my folks crazy. But I found it a challenge."

"Interesting. Did you do any painting in Vietnam?"

"A little, mostly oils."

"I've got to see them. War scenes?"

"No," he said flatly. "I'll show you sometime."

"Promise?"

"Yes," he laughed, "Come on, we're getting way too somber or maybe way too sober. Let's get back to tequila and margaritas and hope the band can play something that we know ." He lifted the dish of limes up as a signal to the bartender and two glasses of tequila showed up instantly.

"Welcome this evening," called out the guitar player and the crowd began to settle in around the tables and fill the few spaces at the bar. "In honor of the tequila drinkers in the corner, we're going to start out with a little Jimmy Buffet. Here it is, Margaritaville just for you." Domino had it right. The band was first rate. The music delivered a crisp Key West beat while two people amused themselves with each others wrists and lime juice and salt and straight shots of tequila. But when Pencil Thin Mustache and Grapefruit-Juicy Fruit came along, they hurried out to the dance floor to add a couple more bodies to the Buffet boogie beat.

Then just as quickly as the band began Buffet, it changed the tempo altogether and pulled out the country with Waylon and Willie. They lingered on the floor through an entire set, swaying to the twangs of the 'cryin in your beer' music , the red dress melding into a cradle of khaki.

"How bout a little Patsy Kline?" shouted a burly bearded guy seated at the bar.

"Here's Crazy just for you," responded the guitar player.

"Not for me, for these two," he addressed Jack and Gage. As he spoke, he turned to Gage and lifted her up onto the bar and pushed the stool over to Jack, who followed suit stepping up alongside her.

"Hit em' again with a round of drinks, " Jack called out to the bartender as Gage took off her shoes and they began to dissolve slowly into the sultry beat of the oldie. He kissed her bare shoulder, nudging the tiny strap until it fell helplessly on her arm. She moistened her fingers and ran them across his lips and he touched them gently with his tongue. They became the music. Not just the music in the little bistro, but music from a place that they could only reach together. The deliberate and provocative rhythm fueled an explosion of earthy sensuality. It pushed those gathered in the humid, backlighted dance area to voice their approval with foot stomping and high decibel whistles.

" Isn't this a scene out of an old Rita Hayworth movie?" she shouted over the clamor of the drinkers as the music ended.

"Yep, and the elephants stampede pretty soon. Time to get out of here."

He thanked the bar crowd for their hospitality and the burly big guy helped them down from their stage, shook their hands and told them that they'd made his evening. Jack guided her gently through the haze of smoke and candlelight. "Hey," he began and then paused as they made their way through the jumbled tables.

"Before you finish, just to save an awkward moment.... the answer's yes. There's an old.... but interesting hotel around the block."

He threw his head back in a long low chuckle. "Yeah, I know, I made a reservation there this afternoon."

"What?"

"Well, if you'd said no, I'd have been too depressed to drive back to St. Louis tonight anyway."

"Then what about the reservation that I made?"

"Oh no, McClendon, you didn't," he teased. He was surprised and pleased and disbelieving, a little.

"Did I?" she shot back.

"Well, if you did, thanks… thanks… I'm overwhelmed and delighted. I've got to settle up with the bar." He lifted her legs on to the chair that he'd been sitting in earlier. "Sit still a minute, and we'll walk to the hotel."

The minute turned into ten minutes as the adding machine ran its register tape around and down the bar station clicking off food and drinks and more drinks. Looking over her shoulder, Gage watched the ease with which Jack moved and talked with these strangers. The guy had such unpretentious charisma.

10

It was late, it was warm and it was humid. It was supposed to be, it was late August. With her shoes slung over her shoulder and their arms around each others waists, they walked and laughed and stopped and talked. She felt a rekindling of responsiveness that she hadn't felt in a long time, and he kept a reality check, a kind of 'pinch me...see if I'm dreaming' check, going on in his head. Except for the magnification of the occasional street light, the two clinging silhouettes could have passed for teen age lovers.

"Look," Gage whispered. They stopped as she pointed to a window on the dark side of the hotel. On the second story with a dim light in the background was a nude woman framed in the dark surrounds of a window. The figure stood fixed in one spot for a few moments and then shifted positions, once propping her elbows on the ledge and leaning forward so that her pendulous breasts swung across the window sill and another time turning slowly sideways to cast the profile of a ghostly delineation. They stepped into a door recess and watched tacitly. It wasn't long until an explanation stepped from between the tall hedges into the narrow street.

"I guess that takes it out of the spooky category... a man, a camera... and a model. Little towns have artistic entitlements too," Jack acknowledged as they waited in the shadows until the photographer disappeared inside the hotel. "And so, pilots and art gallery directors also have artistic license." With that he pulled Gage close, so close that their bodies created a suction in the moist night air. He lifted her off the ground and they twirled in circles, laughing as they fell on the thick damp grass. They were two people fueled in a small part by tequila but mostly buoyed by a natural high. Their silliness erupted in little spasms of snickerings which they tried to contain in a smothering of kisses.

"This is for Vietnam," she said attempting a amateurish salute.

"And this is for the Louisiana Purchase," he interrupted her salute and quieted her giddiness with complete contact of his mouth.

"What the hell's the Louisiana Purchase got to do with anything," she sputtered.

"If I've got my history right, this town was probably a French outpost and as such was part of the Louisiana Purchase."

"And? that's it... just that the town was part of the Louisiana Purchase," she postured a patronizing stance, only to be quickly leveled by a loud hiccup. "Okay, forget the history lesson, let's go inside, I need a drink of water."

"Let's go anyway before we get arrested for PDL."

"Say again."

"Public display of lust," he shrugged. More snickering, enough to make them realize that they needed to stop and compose themselves before they entered the hotel. Inside, a combination of old leather and pungent spices hovered around the registry desk. Or, perhaps it was cherry pipe tobacco, there was a well worn pipe lying in a tray on the counter. The patina of age darkened wood and the ambrosia of vintage scents set a powerful ambience.

"Reservation for Callahan," Jack said softly so as not to disturb the night clerk's solitude. The old gentleman wasn't asleep, but he wasn't wide awake either.

"Yes sir, I was beginning to think you were a no show."

"I wouldn't think you'd have much of a no show problem here."

"Sometimes we do, and sometimes we don't. Tonight it looks like we have a couple more no shows," the clerk responded looking down on a hand written page.

"Tell me, was one of the names on the... never mind". He thought for a second and decided to go with not knowing for sure. A glance showed her intently studying the room roster.

"Room's on the second floor. Room 14, lucky number. A man staying in that room won the lottery once. You folks have a nice night."

They thanked him and headed toward the stairs. Room 14 was at the end of a narrow corridor. As they passed a beveled mirror over a console table in the hall, they both gasped. "I don't know how that poor old man at the desk kept a straight face," Gage exclaimed. "We look pathetic. I have leaves in my hair, there are grass stains all over your shirt, and it looks like we're wearing wet clothes."

Jack unlocked the door with the old fashioned key and they stepped into another era. For a guy whose off duty time was spent mostly in hotels....with work out rooms and lap top connections, it was like walking into a billeting time warp. The oak furnishings were probably 1920's. The serpentine oak dresser looked like something out of everybody's idea of a grandmother's house. Gage walked around the room pausing to touch an ironstone pitcher and bowl decorated with cobalt blue daffodils. Her Chicago apartment was pickled birch and glass.

"This looks like a movie set," she muttered. "Okay, you pretend you're a biplane barnstormer and I'll be your 'lil flapper sweetheart' and we'll be in the proper time frame."

He smiled at her. She knew that her chatter was a way to fill an ungraceful moment. She walked toward her old friend, "Well then, pretend we have music and you ask me to dance."

"Okay," he went along with the ruse. "What kind of music shall we pretend to have?"

She rolled her tongue in a vibrating trill, raised an eyebrow and said playfully, "Ravel's Bolero, maybe."

At that, he curtsied in a broad low sweep and then took her in his arms, "Have you?"

"No," she confessed.

"Well, perhaps you might want to tone down your expectations just a tad."

"Don't think so," she said without hesitancy as she ran her fingers around the back of his neck. "You and that devil tequila have fabricated a Bolero state of mind ." She swung around turning her back to him and he slowly unzipped the summer dress and let it fall to the floor. Then swooping it up, he swirled it around and flung it up on the old ceiling fan where it went round and round adding to the Bolero mystique. She unbuttoned his shirt and let her hands probe evocatively along the taunt chest muscles. She circled his nipples with her fingers and felt the firmness of the response. He reached for her arms and lowered them to her side so he could lift her breasts and pull her into his mouth with all the passion of the years that he'd missed. The floor fell heir to discarded clothes leaving two people free and unfettered to explore those same emotions that Ravel must have drawn from to bring his music to the ultimate explosion of the senses. The physicality was salacious and rapturous and purging. It was the purging of everything outside of 'here and now' that allowed the excessive fires of love making to sustain until the lovers were consumed and the passion demons were quieted. And quiet was a good friend... patient and slow in arriving.

The first light of morning....indeed, the first ray of sun scanned the red dress still moving with the fan blade in a slow steady circle. Gage looked up and smiled, a very relaxed smile. What would those nice salesladies think of the conduct of that red dress in the last twenty four hours? It was good that she'd planned to go on to Chicago from here and had a suitcase in the car. From the bed it looked like that red dress was probably minus one strap.

Jack was already awake. He sensed that she'd just looked up. "I'm sorry about your dress, looks like it got wounded in action. I'll go to your car if you've got other clothes with you." He reached over and pulled her close and they lay quietly under the breeze of the old fan. Neither said much, but it was comfortable and pleasant and they were adrift in an upper zone of serenity when church bells somewhere in the distance reminded them of a world outside the sweep of the crimson clad fan. He stirred, "I've got to check on my plane and you've got an exhibit to finish." He bent down and picked up what appeared to be clothing in the throes of a bad hangover. "No choice, I need these to go to the car."

She scrambled to get her keys and headed straight for the shower. The water felt invigorating and she lingered until she heard the door open. Wrapped only in a big bath towel she felt a tinge of relief at seeing her overnight bag.

"Your phone was on the seat and it kept ringing so I answered it," he chided.

"Who was it?"

"A guy, a guy who asked a hundred questions."

"Probably a friend who is taking care of my cat."

"Gage honey, he wasn't interested in talking about your cat. But hey, I'm a good guy, I told him that you'd call him back. I told him that you'd call him back after we get your dress off the ceiling fan."

"What! You cad!!" She knew he was teasing, nevertheless it was lousy timing. Her mind was racing. Was it better to explain Frank right now, which could take awhile or to spend these last moments focused on now. Now won. After they rescued the dress and Jack finished his shower, they walked around the town square looking for a breakfast diner. "Looks like we're destined for a golden arch breakfast, Major." There was a McDonald's at the interstate exit. They took both cars so they could head out from there.

Biscuits and gravy went down quickly, coffee gave them a little more time to linger. But they knew that the weekend had to end and neither knew what to expect or whether they could expect anything at all. And both were wise enough not to press for answers that were probably not even formulated.

"Got to go, babe. I'll see you in Chicago sometime this week. I'm sure I'm not the first to tell you, but you are one classy dame."

"Thanks," she said rather modestly. As he turned to walk to his car, she called out, "Callahan!"

As he turned he heard with clear intonation, "You're a hunk!"

They both left laughing.

11

His trip back was routine. Think about the plane. Think about her. Think about the plane again. Think about her. It got him back.

Her miles were a little longer, but it was much the same scenario with the exception of Frank. She had to work Frank into her journey. After all, he was her friend… and he did call. She was puzzled at why she was thinking that she had to justify him at all. Somewhere in the St. Louis area she waved a last good bye to the impressive Jaguar and its equally impressive driver. The Sunday traffic was light. She was on cruise and it was time to return Frank's call. She put her cell phone on speaker mode and punched in his number.

"Yea," he answered.

"It's me.

"Ah, fair lady, where are you and who was the dude?"

"I'm on my way home, just north of St. Louis."

"And?"

"First, how's my cat?

"Pancho's cool. Come on, spill it."

"How much time do you have? It's not a five minute story."

"It's Sunday afternoon. The ball game is over. I'm sitting on my balcony alone… not by choice mind you, but alone. So let me have it, I'm ready to hear something hot. Are you okay?"

" I'm just great. Alright, I was in a restaurant in Cape and a guy came in looking for me. Well, first he was in Chicago on business and he saw the article about Mac's exhibit in a tourism package. He called the Gallery and they told him where I'd gone."

"Wait, a minute. What right did he have to come stalking someone that he saw in print?" Frank demanded in his typical offensive manner.

"Well, hold on His name is Jack Callahan. He isn't just any guy. He was a pilot, a hell of a pilot, that I knew casually in Vietnam. We spent Thursday evening together reminiscing." She went on to give a glowing account of their conversation.

"You just talked, huh?" He baited her.

"That night, yes. Later, there was a little town north of here."

He butted in, "You spent the whole weekend with him? Gage girl, I haven't been reading you right."

"Frank, you're frustrating, you know that? It wasn't the whole weekend. He had to be in Atlanta Friday. He came back Saturday afternoon and we met in a little town half way between St. Louis and Cape. Hey, I even bought a new dress."

"New dress brings it to a more serious level," he laughed. " Go on." He didn't want to kid her too much. It had been hard enough to get her to go out at all. So it was surprising to hear her talking so freely.

"Oh Frank, it was surreal. He was incredible. Handsome, after all those years. Kind, funny, exciting... an extraordinary guy. We had dinner in an old French town. There was a band and we danced. Uh... we even danced on the bar," she said coyly. " Gage McClendon straight out of an old Rita Hayworth movie, can you imagine?"

Truth was, he couldn't. He was more than a little surprised. He was dumbfounded. This was the woman that had to be coaxed, even bribed, to go out for dinner if there was to be an unattached male anywhere in the party. "I'm sure you two were a stunning pair. And you spent the night with him," he remarked half heartedly. It was complicated, wanting the best for your friend, but not eager to share her attention.

A glance at the speedometer alarmed her, talking fast and driving fast both. She moved into a slower lane and went on with the conversation. "The food was grand. You'd have loved it. Grilled swordfish and delicate little potato puffs. Such a quaint little place. The full bar took on the flavor of a private party."

"Okay, I got it. What about sex?"

"It wasn't sex," she said adamantly.

"Oh, yea, I forgot... for a woman if it's good sex, it's called making love, right?" He'd been in a brouhaha on that point at various times in the past.

She glossed right over his sarcasm, going on with a glowing chronicle of her evening. The more she talked, the more animated her gestures became. It even crossed her mind that she probably appeared in a curious state of excitability to passerbys, but she continued. She described the walk to the hotel, the holding hands and the kissing in the dark doorway while spying on the lady with the swinging boobs. She led Frank through a visual impression of the old hotel lobby and its long corridor. Cruising down the highway had once again become racing down the highway, so she slacked off both the speed and conversation momentarily.

"What's happening, don't lose me now," Frank yelled, worried that they could be losing phone contact.

"I'm right here. I'm talking too fast and driving too fast. I need a cigarette."

"What are you talking about? You don't even smoke! You're on one hell of a high though. Look I'm trying to follow your story. And my dear, it looks like you reached the prime meridian, the circle of constant longitude, and you had to either cross or step back. So I'm betting that you crossed it."

"Crossed it hell, we remapped it," she shouted. "Frank, I can't believe that I'm telling you this, but on a scale of 1 to 10, last night was at least a 25. It was splendor, it was saucy, it was sexy, it was… well… like… when you're making candy, making fudge, and it's cooking and boiling and bubbling and the aroma is sensual and provocative. Its movement is so awesome, so powerful, it's chocolate dancing. That was last night!" It was as if she had to get it all told in one breath, almost like she was going to hyperventilate if she didn't spit it out quickly. Then she quieted down and slowed down and waited for Frank's reaction.

In the pith of her prattling, there was some real confession and Frank didn't want to mess up with a typical male back slapping response. He knew her. He knew that a fragile sensitivity was at stake and some tightrope walking of emotions would lie ahead. So he took it slowly, answering, "I'm darned pleased for you. The guy has to be the luckiest bloke in the world, of course. And just to hear you so giddy… well, he has my seal of approval."

"Thanks a bunch, though I'm a little surprised at your reserve. I thought you would make chopped liver out of this. What a switch… me, wild and wicked, and you, the pater noster."

"You're right, I've got my brakes on," he admitted. "But if you wanna' do some trash talking, I've got some gutter questions." He really didn't expect a green light on that, and she didn't give him one.

In fact, she ignored his comments and proceeded on a different tangent. "When I get back to the apartment tonight, it'll be too late to call you. So while I've got you on the phone let me tell you what I need for the exhibit. God, it opens Thursday and I've got previews and media promos both Tuesday and Wednesday. Tomorrow will be a long day because I've got to wrap it all up. Can you do the final photos mid to late Wednesday afternoon?"

"It's a deal. Let's grab something to eat afterwards and you can tell me how many times you did it?"

"You're a piece of work, you are. Yes, to dinner. It seems like an eternity since we've had any 'girlfriend' time."

"Don't call me girlfriend. My testosterone levels are the bar that set the standards," he replied lightheartedly. I've already fed Pancho today and cleaned the litter box, good guy that I am. By the way, your neighbor Mrs. Giovanni, is a little strange. I think she keeps trying to come on to me and doesn't have the slightest idea of how one goes about that sort of thing. Mama, mia, I can't imagine anyone in the whole world getting excited over those flowered house dresses and giant yellow daisy earrings."

"Mrs. Giovanni? No way. She's a little quirky but she'd never make a play for you, or anybody for that matter. You misread her... bless her heart."

Frank stayed his ground. "I know moves and that old gal was trying some."

"Jeesh, Frank, she's a little old lady who lives in the past and would just like a little attention, that's all. She's got a heart as big as those plastic earrings. Maybe, you flatter yourself too much, huh, big guy?" Mrs. Giovanni... nah, that's kooky! See you soon, Frank, bye, bye."

"Give me a break," he moaned. "Talk later."

The last part of the trip was tiring, heavier traffic and exits closer together. She had to concentrate on driving, but the vision of a shriveled up Mrs. Giovanni in her muu muu trying to put the make on Mr. Fashion Plate himself was substantial enough to keep replaying again and again in her mind.

If Frank was right, was it because he was Italian? Mrs. G. was Italian and Milano was her center of the universe. Her husband had taken her half way around the world in search of la dolce vita. But it wasn't just the good life that she wanted, it was the good Italian life and as such she never let poor Mr. Giovanni forget it. He stayed out of her way most of the time. Yet, at times she'd seen some tender moments between them.

All lanes were jammed with short tempered drivers as Gage got closer to the city. The fortunates were returning from weekend outings and they were tired and reluctant to give up their play time. Fatigue had definitely become a major player by the time she pulled into her parking garage.

Pancho Sanchez was waiting where he always waited, under a tall flower arrangement on the stand table near the door. Mac always said that Pancho could hear her car four stories down in the garage. "You're a good fellow. Come on, I've missed you." She turned toward a chair and before she could be seated, he was there walking right up her chest to look her in the eye. She intended to ask him what he knew about Frank and Mrs. Giovanni, but they both quickly drifted into a peaceful purring slumber.

12

Jack spent Sunday afternoon hanging out with the avionics techs who were working on his plane. It looked like it was going to run into evening before they were finished, so he decided to take a shuttle to one of the motels across from the airport. He had an idea and he thought he was okay on time. He had to get the plane to its new owners by Friday and he'd promised Gage that he would see her this week. He was pretty sure that the exhibit was to open on Thursday, so he figured that he should probably try to see her Wednesday. Thursday, she'd belong to the art world.

He checked into a budget motel across from the airport, got a bucket of ice, a bottle of water and stretched out on the bed. It felt good to get off the concrete hangar floor. He picked up the phone and dialed a Wyoming number that he had called hundreds of times from hundreds of places.

"Hello," it was a robust but friendly voice.

"Sis, are you busy right now or can you talk?" She was always busy, worked way too hard. She took on the ranch after their folks died and never took time for a life of her own. He'd tried to get her to pull back some, but keeping the place productive had become her passion.

"Hey, always got time for you, big guy. What's up? Didn't know you were in the country."

"I'm going to sell my plane later this week, but I'd like to fly you to Laramie in the Baron for dinner one last time. I'll be in sometime tomorrow afternoon. How's the strip?"

"It's good. The cattle have it cropped pretty close." When Jack was a teenager, their dad cleared some scrub trees and set aside a long level section of a pasture for a landing strip. Then he'd wait for the boy to fly out from the airport with his instructor and proudly watch as the young aviator shot touch and go's time and time again. Forty years later, it was still called the strip. " I'll listen for you, bud."

Pliny was the only other Callahan left. She stayed at home until it was too late to leave. Both parents came to depend on her business acumen. In fact, their mother insisted that she'd willed her baby daughter to be brilliant by naming her after a first century Roman scholar. Neither parent had ever heard the name articulated, so they pronounced it like the word plenty, without the t.

"Okay, I'll buzz you. Hasta mañana." He rolled over, placed the phone back on the table and his next conscious movement was to shield his eyes from the morning sun.

He looked at the clock and decided it was time to come alive again, then headed for the shower while stripping off yesterday's clothes. A glance outside, instinctively the first thing he did every morning, and it looked bright and blue. He finished up, went to the lobby and grabbed the complimentary breakfast, a danish and coffee, and checked out.

The plane was ready and he inspected it thoroughly. It had been a good friend to him and he wanted to make sure it stayed healthy. Lambert had a long wait for take offs, but he finally got in the air and headed for cowboy country. He never tired looking at the farmland below. It always looked like it had been laid out with a tape measure, precision square corners and long perfectly straight borders. There was a lot of quality thinking time in this kind of flying. And he did a lot of thinking. All about Chicago, all about a Ms. Gage B. McClendon, a gal who probably had no idea how she transfused his entire cerebral and physical system. A gal who probably had the right stuff to actually ground him. Immediately, he scolded himself out loud, "Fool, what the hell, are you thinking." Scolding worked for a moment....only a moment, but the thought of actually having a permanent address instead of a post office box was a bit jolting. So he concentrated on the broad expanse of rural America looking like a geographical patchwork quilt from the air.

He could see cattle standing idly along the little crooked creek, then the barns and finally the old homestead. He came in low enough that he noticed a few shingles missing on the northwest corner of the house. One pass over the place was all that was ever needed to send Pliny to the pasture to pick him up. A little bumpy, but what the heck, it was a convenient landing strip and as he turned and taxied toward the house, he could see Pliny, tanned and smiling in her old truck.

Her hair with its gray streaks and sun streaks mingled together gave her an extra healthy look. He felt a little guilty that she'd never really had the opportunity to meet a right guy, she would have made a great mate, always upbeat and happy. She had a lot of close friends, it wasn't as if she lived a hermit's life so far out of town, and this time he even noticed a satellite dish on the house.

"Welcome home, bud," she called out as the propeller noise whined down. He opened the door and jumped down right into the most genuine hug that would melt a mother's heart to see one sibling give another sibling.

"Plin, you look great. It's so good to see you. I've missed you, girl."

"Well, little brother, you look pretty damn great, yourself. Come on, I've got a ranch hand supper ready for you. It's a little early to eat, but with all the catching up, we can eat and talk all evening."

The old house was like a time warp. Pliny was too busy with chores and bookkeeping to get caught up in decor and decorating. He carried his flight bag up the stairs and into his old room. He hated to think of it as such, but his room looked more like a shrine to him than a place for a guy to relax. His old softball and basketball pictures in frames were still sitting on a weary looking chest of drawers. College pennants on the wall, a Marilyn Monroe calendar on the back of the door, the memories came flooding back. Pliny came up to see if she could help him and they chatted on and on, mostly about their childhood and the fond memories of their parents. And how two such very quiet people turned out two very strong willed children.

"Are the paintings still here that I shipped back from Viet Nam?" he asked.

"Yes, they're in the back of the big closet in the hall," she said going to the door. She opened it to show him. Sure enough, they were there still wrapped in the heavy shipping paper.

"I'm going to take a couple of them back with me this time."

"Do you still paint? You always had the darndest way of painting. You'd want us to put little groupings of things together for you to paint, yet when we would look at your painting it was never what we put together. If we put an orange, you could bet that when you finished it was orange peel in a long winding spiral and a knife or something. You always insisted that you were painting ahead of time... what something would look like later on. I think you stretched Mom's patience on that issue."

"I suppose I did. But it seemed perfectly logical to me. Enough of this, let's go test your cooking. Gee, Sis, how do you keep so trim?" he kidded as they entered the kitchen. "Or do you run a boarding house on the side?" There was food everywhere. Then his eye caught the table set with three place settings. Uh, oh, he did a mental assessment, Pliny's invited a girl friend, it seemed they were always just divorced or just about to get divorced. He wished she wouldn't do it but it seemed to give her a little one up on her friends. "Are we having company, Pliny?"

"JC, I need to explain something, okay? I'm not getting any younger or stronger and those darn calves were wearing me out. So, I hired someone to help me out."

"Good job, you should have done it long ago."

"Hear me out, he's become a very important part of my life."

"I'm beginning to get the picture, Plin. It's great, I'm happy for you," he reassured her. It wasn't to say that he wasn't surprised. There's something about hearing your sister say she's living with someone, or in this case, someone's living with her that shakes you for a second. "Where is your guy, and what's his name? Let's meet him."

"His name is Raven Tall Wing, that's his Indian name. His other name is Curtiss Markham."

"Sioux?"

"His mother is Sioux and his father was a Union Pacific Railroad worker. He left when Curt was a baby. I think you'll like him, Jack. He's witty and hardworking and handsome."

The timing was good because just as she finished, the door opened and Curt came in carrying a puppy which had been abandoned up the road. He took time to say hello and shook hands and then hand fed the little mongrel as they talked. It would be hard to not like someone who was so gentle and kind to the limpid mass of brown fuzz curled up in his hands. It also gave Jack time to size him up. He was rugged and strong and handsome with his black-silver hair, just as his sister had described.

Curt finished with the puppy and placed it on a towel near the door. Then, as if anticipating questions that Jack might have, he gave a rundown of his life and told Jack how much Pliny meant to him and soon they were laughing and eating and drinking a toast with home made elderberry wine... powerful elderberry wine.

"The satellite dish," Jack mused out loud.

" We like to watch foreign movies," Pliny butted in. "Curt's a real movie afficionado. Why he even had a bit part in a movie that was shot in Cheyenne." He saw Curt flinch so he thought it best not to go there. More power to them. After seven or eight toasts, Jack was beginning to wilt so he excused himself and started upstairs. It had been a long day and in a way, a very contented day. He really was happy that Pliny wasn't alone any longer. He slept until the aroma of bacon overtook his sleep. There was always a smorgasbord of breakfast foods in this house. There always had been, and it looked like Pliny was keeping the tradition alive. He dressed and went down. His sister was leaving to go out to the tractor as he came into the kitchen so she stopped and poured each of them a cup of coffee. She pulled his breakfast off the warming burner and sat down with him. She expected some questions.

"That was some bombshell you dropped... you and Curt. How long have you been together?"

"About six months, shortly after you were here last. It's kind of late in life, I know. But we are really happy together. He's a kind and compassionate person, hey, and he's romantic too."

"Gonna tie the knot?" he pried modestly.

"When you do," she tossed back.

" You know, it's a hoot, my sister living here in sin. Mom and Pop would have been beside themselves."

"But, of course, if Mom and Pop were here, you can bet I wouldn't be living here....in sin, as you say." They laughed. Laughter was a bond between them. "What about you? Is there anybody in your life?"

"I don't know, Sis. There is a gal from Viet Nam days. I've just run into her again and I'm going to Chicago tomorrow to see her. With me, that's pretty serious. So, we'll see." He quickly finished eating and asked her to point him to wherever Curt was working. He wanted to help out and get to know his almost brother-in-law. She smiled, it meant a lot to her that Jack was open to her relationship. He hopped on the back of the tractor and they headed out to the west pasture where Curt was busy working with a calf that had gotten mangled in a fight with a pack of stray dogs.

"I'm a little rusty at ranching but I work cheap," Jack volunteered.

The rugged outdoorsman looked up and with a twinkle in his eye said, "You're on." They worked and talked and sweated. And drank water and worked some more and took a break when Pliny brought lunch out to them. By quitting time, Jack had to agree with his sister, Raven Walking Tall Curt was genuine and he could see why she had fallen for him.

By sundown, they were all cleaned up and ready to go to Laramie. Pilots take for granted that the rest of the world uses the airways like they do... all the time. So Jack was stunned when Curt mentioned rather humbly that he'd never been in a plane. How long ago had it been since he'd flown a first timer. "Come on, cowboy, let's get you in the air so you won't be the last person in North America to fly." They piled in the plane, Curt looking a bit unsure of his fate but being a good sport about it. The evening was beautiful and after the lumpy pasture was below them, the air was as smooth as glass and the new flier kept the other two entertained with his exclamations of astonishments. From the air, Jack called the tower to ask that a taxi meet them to shuttle them into town to the old steak house where they went each time Jack came home.

Belle was a real creation, one of a kind. She'd been a waitress at the steak house as long as anyone could remember, except for a short time when she was a pit boss at a casino in Vegas. She said she came back to Laramie because the people in Vegas were too soft. "What you doin' in town, Ace?" she said in the whiskey throated voice that befitted her nickname 'Bar Room Belle'. "Last I heard, you were about to get hitched to some socialite from Grosse Pointe, Michigan."

"You heard wrong Belle, I'm waiting for you."

"Waitin' is the key word, sonny boy. Come see me in say, twenty years."

"What a woman," he whistled. She was at least seventy-five years old and as witty as they come. Everybody knew Belle and Belle knew everybody.

"By the way, what did happen to the Grosse Pointe dame?" Pliny questioned.

" M.P. Logan... Martha Patricia Logan, well I suspect that by now she's married to some poor corporate slob and she's still going to 1950's tea parties. That whole episode lasted two weeks at the most, how in hell did Belle know about it?"

"Oh, probably through Claire or Cass. By the way, I forgot to tell you they'll both be here shortly."

"Pliny, give up on it," he said pretending to groan. "I thought the third plate on the table last night was for one of the girls and when it wasn't I thought I'd beaten the odds on your matchmaking." Claire and Cass were Pliny's closest friends. Claire had been divorced for years, never talked much about it and Cass was married to a miner that everybody called Pick. He had died of lung cancer about ten years ago. Pliny's warning wasn't any too soon, Jack saw their reflections in the mirror over the bar. Claire had on enough make-up to at least get her noticed but poor pitiful pearl Cass needed a complete overhaul.

"Hi, handsome," Claire gurgled. Nothing shy here. She edged Cass out of her way and seated herself solidly at his side.

"Hello, girls," he tried to act as eager to see them as he could. He caught Pliny looking much too gleeful. How many times had she set this little scenario up over the years? Not much to do but play it out, they traded greetings for a short time and then Belle ratcheted up the tempo while taking their orders. She told them that he'd come to town to find a woman. He could almost see the antennas telescoping and he saw Curt stifle a chuckle. What babes, these two, but he wouldn't want to let Pliny down so he bantered around every subject that he thought they might be interested in. Even then they always brought the subject back to him... Where are you based?... Is there a love interest?... Do you plan on coming back here when you retire?... And, same question again, is there a love interest?

"Okay, Okay, right now I'm flying out of Indonesia, I'm still delivering food and much needed medicines. I haven't made any retirement plans yet, and, let's see there was another question, wasn't there?" he might as well make their interest obvious. "Oh yes, I believe it was, is there a love interest? Now who in their right mind would want a guy who doesn't even have an address, who lives out of a suitcase?"

No answer from either, only snickering, and the questions didn't stop. "Have you ever had any close calls?" Clair continued. "Like when you thought that you might not make it."

"Not in the air. Once some junkies hit me up for money to buy yaba and then for a few minutes I thought it might be the end of the road. But they were happy with my watch and my money and I was able to walk away, a bit shaken... well a lot shaken, actually. But knock on something, I've been fortunate."

"Yaba?" Cass had a blank look.

"Speed."

"Oh," she replied offhandedly.

The meal went along nicely, the steak was a bona fide treat. The girls weren't really any trouble. Pliny and Curt sat close together touching each other devotedly. The evening finally came to a close. Jack picked up the check. Therefore, the girls thought the least they could do would be to drive them out to the airport. Cass drove them right up to the plane, and they oohed and aahed over it so pathetically, that he felt obligated. "Come on gals, everybody in, there's room for us all." They were actually a lot of fun in a comedic type way. Their mouths didn't close from the time they taxied out on to the runway to the fifteen minute flyover of the town. "Hey, it's just a little plane for Christ's sakes. What do you do when you get in a commercial jet?"

Pliny shouted over the chatter, "I think it would depend on who the pilot is."

"Gotcha," he laughed and turned back toward the airport. He figured that he might just as well follow through with this mutual admiration society and he gave each one of them a quick kiss as he let them out on the ground.

"Ye doggies, that'll be good for five years worth of beauty shop talk," Curt chimed in.

The night ended quietly with the girls gone. Jack spent a little time talking to his sister about the ranch and then rescued a couple of paintings from the hall closet so he wouldn't forget them in the morning. He thanked Curt for being right for Pliny and turned in. He had to get back out into the other world, that comfortable world of wings and wanderings. It just wasn't of much interest to him that it takes ten acres to feed one cow. Everybody has a place somewhere, he wasn't sure exactly where his was, but he was sure where it wasn't.

Early the next morning he did a thorough walk around, checked everything very carefully and hopped in the plane. Ready for take off, he opened the door and gave Curt and Pliny a thumbs up as he taxied along the cow pasture. Glancing over his shoulder to make sure the paintings that he tied behind a seat were going to fly okay, he lifted off. Destination... 'Chi' town.

13

Monday was hectic. Gage hauled the paintings from Missouri into the Gallery. A couple of them needed some cleaning and one of the most outstanding oils had a tiny tear in the corner. The restoration people were going to go ballistic. Even so, in the long run they would come through. Before every opening they would swear that this was the last time they were going to bust their butts in the final hours. On the other hand they recognized that it was a collective effort and they were just venting. Nevertheless, she didn't relish marching into their area with last minute restoration work.

They didn't let her down. They fussed and fumed and then acquiesced quietly and went to work. She left them to hover over the project and went to her office to try and catch up on the messages. Greta met her in the hall. "Morning, Greta. Oh, please don't tell me those are all mine," she winced, looking at the message sheets in the receptionist's hand. " Not now, not today, I don't have time."

"Well, I think we better take time. A couple of them are calls from board members wanting to know how everything's going and there's probably a dozen print and radio media wanting you to call them. How was your weekend?"

The question startled Gage. How did she know? Whoops, guilty conscience, it was just a polite inquiry. "It was fine, Greta, just fine." She resigned herself to sorting out the messages before she could get to her primary task, that of opening a first class exhibit three days from now. She had a tough time sitting through what turned out to be an entire morning of returning messages.

She couldn't ignore the Board of Directors. Those two came first on the return calls and neither one seemed to be in any hurry to get off the phone. They were no trouble, merely wanted to be a part of the process, be involved. The media was a different story. They wanted to be involved too, but in a more avaricious way. Greta helped by heading off some of the periphery calls. She'd worked with Gage long enough to know which media groups to take seriously. Between the two of them, they worked the phones all day. The show was taking on a real air of excitement in the city. Mac was being hailed as 'a Chicago treasure' and hyped all over the press.

The entire day was the cacophony she'd anticipated. Evening came and the gallery lights were off before she realized that she hadn't gotten a chance to see the finishing touches that everyone had been working on so diligently. She grabbed some homework, stuffed it in her briefcase and headed for the door toward the welcome quiet of her own private art world. It was usually a very short drive to her apartment, but this evening there were detours having to do with some kind of emergency work on underground water lines. Add thirty minutes more to the usual fifteen minute drive and night was rapidly crowding her evening at home.

The next morning she was determined to take control of the day rather than allow the day to take control of everything in its path. Shortly after arriving at work, she grabbed a cup of coffee and made the rounds of the display areas before workers with hammers and tape measures and other auspicious looking instruments worked their final magic on the exhibition. As she looked at the brilliant, bold strokes... very contemporary and yet so very warm, she marveled at the insight and the talent of the man she'd lived with and loved with all those wonderful years. Would it ever stop, would she ever be able to look at that familiarity and not feel the hurt and anguish at losing him? And now suddenly, there was another emotion to contend with... betrayal. "No," she admonished herself, "I refuse to go there." But in the back of her mind, she worried that even thinking the word gave it inception.

"Gage, can you come meet with Beryl Paschal in ten minutes?" came Greta's voice quietly from behind.

" Absolutely." No one in the art world would say no to Beryl Paschal. She was the art critic from hell. Even if she liked your show, you got scathing critical reviews. But if she didn't like it, she could banish you so fast your shadow would have to run to catch up with you. Gage returned to the office to prepare for the Paschal inquisition and to settle from the disquieting moments in the gallery.

The staccato footsteps of the matron of malcontent struck the terrazo floors like a jack hammer. "Good morning, Mrs. McClendon." Continuing without a break for a return greeting allowed her to dominate a conversation, and she used the intimidation tactic very effectively. When Beryl Paschal left your presence you always wanted to bang your head on the wall at your ineptness in dealing with her. "Walk me through the show, give me the spiel and answer some questions."

Naught to do, but follow along. A good review was worth a little humiliation of the soul. Gage guided her from room to room explaining each painting's raison d'etre to the best of her ability. As they neared the third room of the collection, she sensed a softer intonation in the inquiries. She wondered if deep down in that cast iron framework, there might actually be a soft spot.

"The collection is important," she acknowledged and closed her notebook. That was the entire summation of a forty five minute walk through. It almost made Gage sick to her stomach, she wanted so desperately to pull more from this power player. They walked to the big Gallery doors and without breaking stride, Beryl Paschal turned to her quiet hostess and gently touched her on the shoulder. "This couldn't have been easy for you, but it is an exemplary exhibit." And with that she swept through the door in the patent abruptness that had become her trademark.

Gage waited until the door was solidly closed. "It's exemplary, it's exemplary, that's an A+," she called out to no one in particular and skipped a couple of Wizard of Oz steps on the way back to her office. She told Greta and Greta told everyone. The confidence level, which is always a bit shaky before an opening, took a timely upturn. The press folks who were scheduled for the rest of the afternoon as well as those for tomorrow morning were now a piece of cake.

And indeed, it took the rest of the afternoon for rounds with the media and after having been on her feet all day, she looked forward to kicking off her shoes and cooling her feet on the terrazzo. Enter Elliott Brandenberg... the handsome Elliott Brandenberg, sitting on her desk waiting.

"Great job, you've got a winner again," he grinned. She and Elliott had been friends going back a long way, when she was a fledgling 'art beat' reporter and he was an apprentice sports writer.

"Hey, guy, how are you?" she excused herself and pulled her shoes off. "Nice to see you." It ran through her mind that the visit might be more than just a preview of Mac's work. He'd asked her out a few months ago and she'd used the excuse that she was working long hours on this exhibit. He was the kind of guy who could send a female into cardiac flutter....trim, polite, yet capable of a sailor's vocabulary and darn it, there was a earthy sexiness about him.

"It's good to see you, too," he beamed. "As always, you look fantastic. Got a proposition for you. The Cubs will be on the road for the next three nights, so I won't be back in town until Saturday. But is it okay to call you Saturday afternoon? And dammit, Gage, it's time to let down that invisible shield you've girdled around you."

"Just cut to the chase, huh, Ell?" She lauded his play on words and tried to think whether this was the right time to tell him about Jack. There were quick second thoughts on that. She hadn't even told Greta who was still at the computer in the next room, so she stumbled around in framing a sentence and finally came out with, "Oh, I can't I've already got plans for this weekend."

"Tell me those plans don't include another man and you're off the hook. However, sweetheart, if you've let some hairy old ape into my territory, beware the wounded male syndrome."

"What's the wounded male syndrome?"

"It's raving at the top of your lungs before you slink off broken hearted into the forest to die all alone," he gestured dramatically. "And by not eagerly accepting my invite, you've already bruised my ego, so rather than find out for sure whether I have to go to the forest, I'm going to play it safe and revisit this scenario in a couple of weeks. Is that okay with you?"

"You're a dear, have a nice time," she waltzed around an answer. Back when they'd worked together through long late hours and in very close quarters, he was always a gentleman.

"Hey, but don't jack around with me, I won't just go away." Gage turned to face him. He was smiling, but the inflection of his voice wasn't in sync with the smile. He threw her a kiss and sauntered out of the office. A shiver surfaced in little ripples, but there were too many details before wrap-up to spend much time on off-handed comments. Nevertheless, Elliott's remarks and tone of voice stayed with her.

"Is everything okay?" Greta asked coming in on the heels of Elliott's departure. She was generally one to stay out of everybody else's business, but this time and for her friend's well being, she felt that she needed to voice a concern. "I think he sounded threatening."

"No, it was alright, he was smiling. Guys have a strange way of relating, sometimes," Gage mumbled halfheartedly.

They went on for another hour catching up on mail that had piled up while she'd been in Missouri. They chatted away, mostly incidental idle talk. Gage didn't mention Jack. She thought she'd wait until Mac's exhibit was over. For some reason, she didn't feel up to a weighty conversation. She felt a lot more up tight than usual. There were always pre-opening jitters, and this show, in particular, had elevated the stress level.

As they were sifting through the last batch of mail, Greta couldn't hold back, "Mike left me," she said in a very detached manner.

"What? Why didn't you say something sooner? Oh, I'm so sorry! What happened?" Gage was blatantly shocked. Greta and Mike had been married over twenty years. He came to the office to pick her up occasionally and they seemed perfectly suited for each other. In fact, everyone in the office kidded about wanting a marriage that would 'take' like Greta and Mike's. "Mike went to his high school reunion in Cleveland last month. I didn't go because both boys had soccer games they didn't want to miss. We decided he shouldn't miss the reunion, so he went alone. Well, big mistake!" she accentuated the word ' big'. "He changed after he came back, always on his cell phone and not making it to the kids' games. Then last weekend I came home from Brian's game and there was a note on the kitchen table. He left me for his high school sweetheart." She was much too calm for this kind of divulgence, either she was on medication or the hurt was so deep that she wasn't yet bringing the emotions to the surface.

"Let's go grab a beer and pizza," Gage could see she desperately needed some kind of comfort. "How about the boys?"

"The sitter's still there and quite honestly, I could use a friendly ear. I haven't even told my folks yet. Okay, let's go."

She had certainly been a silent sufferer. Gage had been too busy to notice, perhaps, but Greta hadn't given one clue that her world had been turned upside down. They walked a couple of blocks to an old style pizzeria and ordered a couple of beers and a pizza supreme. Greta talked and Gage listened. Gage heard more about Mike than she ever cared to hear and at one time almost dozed in the midst of a sentence that began with Mike, continued on about Mike for at least five minutes, and no less, ended with Mike. The poor girl needed to get it out though, so there was nothing else to do but sit still and wait for tears or tiredness to wind her down.

Two hours into the pizza connection and seemingly more unburdened, Greta thanked her patient listener and gathered up the left overs, "The kids will have eaten, but there's always room for pizza." They walked back to the parking area and Gage made Greta promise to call her anytime she needed to talk.

Pancho Sanchez was waiting... he had no great traumas or dilemmas to impart, just unconditional silent loyalty. He bolted ahead of her to the refrigerator. The big kitty was a delight, just feed him and love him.... simple gratifying pleasure. It's when you add the element of human emotion that life gets snarled in complexities. Gage put a Julio Iglesias CD in the player, all in Spanish, she didn't want to hear anything that she could understand. The sweet soft sounds of rolling r's were her last recall until the shrill of the telephone the next morning.

14

Frank's signature greeting, "Hey," followed by, "any change in the time you want to do the shoot this afternoon?"

"Hi Frank," she glanced up at the clock and turned the CD player off. Enough Julio, thank you. "If we do the session at four o'clock, I should be at the end of the media blitz. Probably will take about an hour and then we can do something, if you still have the time."

"Plenty of time for you gal, this has been a crazy week. And I haven't had a complete accounting of your weekend. By the way, is the mystery man coming to the exhibit?"

"I think so, I'm counting on it. He said he'd see me later this week."

"That's my girl, you said it , you said you're counting on it. For you, that's planetary, that's monumental."

"Come on Frank, you haven't even heard the whole story."

"Oh, I heard plenty... sex by any other name is chocolate dancing. Powerful adjectives, Ms. McClendon."

"Okay, enough," her words came back sounding a little foolish. Maybe foolish out of context, but she could personally justify every syllable of that description. "See you at four, Frankie," she said laughing as she got even with him via the nickname that was guaranteed to annoy.

"Oh, please!" he feigned wounded.

The day before an opening was freakish at the best and bizarre at the worst. She couldn't second guess this one. Greta's problems didn't help, and in some inexplicable way Elliott muddied the mix. So, as she always did, she prepared mentally for the worst, and hoped desperately for a break.

Greta was not a part of the break that she was hoping for. She was down, way down and it was obvious. The miserable Greta couldn't help it, but for the starting point of the day to already have tension in the air was not a good sign. Maybe distraction would work, she called to Greta to help her double check the title and date tags on the paintings for one last time. A good thing too, one of the oils was listed as a gouache. There wasn't a gouache in the show. One of the dates read 1890 instead of 1990. These were muck ups that weren't caught in close scrutiny yesterday. That's when you feel the shoulders tighten and the tummy draw.

There were still a few press people to court and friends of some of the board members getting a one up on the public. A frantic call from one of the floor crew came over the speakers. Gage hurried to the back of the main floor. The string ensemble that was to play during tomorrow's opening felt they needed a more important placement than the floor crew had provided. The crew wouldn't move them and the strings wouldn't give in, so by the time Gage got to the back of the hall, it looked like the stand off at OK Corral. This one was beyond her powers of persuasion as Exhibition Director. She threw it into the court of the big boss, the Executive Director, Mr. Espinosa. She could tell from the way that he raised his right eyebrow, that he didn't like playing arbitrator either, but there had to be a resolution. She was sure to hear about it later.

She walked away leaving Mr. Espinosa deep in assuaging terminology. Heading back to her office, she heard Greta say to one of the assistants, "I don't care, I just think he's creepy." There was a vase of long stem roses on her desk. Greta grew quiet as Gage plucked the card from its holder. 'You're on my mind', Elliott.

"Damn," was her only utterance. She knew where Greta was coming from with the 'I don't care' statement. Her head as well as her neck and shoulders were really aching now and she headed straight for the cache of weary looking pain relievers in the break room. It was three o'clock and she hadn't even thought about eating, maybe that was it. Nonetheless, Greta's problems hung in the back of her mind and Elliott's ape analogy was troubling, not to mention his demeanor. Jack was the light at the end of the tunnel. His presence was a revitalizing force that she welcomed. She wanted him to be a part of her life. And it was at that moment, she realized what she had consciously validated and the serene contentment she felt with her feelings.

"Hey, girls!" What a glorious sunny sound, the voice of the upbeat and trendy Frank Beccacio. The sight of the handsome Sicilian laden with back packs of camera equipment and an interesting array of tripods drew greetings from all over the gallery. He loved it. Actually, he made it happen. Frank loved being adored and he didn't mind working for the adoration. In fact, he'd honed it to a fine art.

"How's my gal?" he quizzed as he gave Gage a hug that lifted her off the floor. He stopped short and looked at her. "Anything wrong? You seem fragile."

Gage noted his quick evaluation. Fragile was, indeed, the right word for the way she felt. "It's great to see you, it seems like eons. Yes, there's something wrong and I can't quite pinpoint it. I think there are too many influences coming together at one time. Oh, that's silly, ignore it. Come on let me help you set up your equipment."

They worked silently, Frank picking out camera angles and Gage, the capable assistant. They unfolded and unzipped and unpacked. They shot wide and zoomed in and talked all the while. Frank, always full of questions anyway, asked a lot of questions about the paintings. Why did Mac paint the hair turquoise on an Asian girl? And why did he paint a rabbit with stripes? What was he thinking when he painted a corporate board meeting inside a stomach? Gage had a sinking feeling that she may have failed Mac. She should have asked him the questions that Frank was asking her. They'd had a model marriage and an extremely close relationship. Yet, they were wise enough to allow each other a private world. She stayed out of his art world, and he kept out of promotion and exhibition. There was presumed to be plenty of time for questions and answers later on, not the abrupt end to his career. As they went from canvas to canvas photographing the brilliant colors, each painting grew more difficult for her to concentrate on because she was struggling hard to keep her emotions in check. Long extended breaths and intense swallowing took over her focus. It wasn't professional and it wasn't becoming, but it was real and it was deep.

15

Tower kept the plane in a holding pattern for fifteen minutes before giving clearance to land and with time cut close, the circles around the sky seemed forever. Hopefully, the paperwork was in order for quick transfer of the Beechcraft to the new owners. Signatures and a final inspection was all that was needed, and of consequential importance of course, their cashier's check. The plane was free and clear of any liens and, apparently they didn't plan on any outside financing, so it made for a clean and easy sale.

He taxied in close to the building, he could see them waiting. They looked proud and eager to take over their new treasure. He shut down, gathered his flight bag and a few other personal items and stepped out of the Baron for the last time. It wasn't easy to look back, akin to leaving an old friend. Greetings and handshakes finished, they went into a little snack bar and had a cup of coffee. They laid out the paperwork while a pilot and a mechanic did an in-depth check of the plane. Everything satisfied and everyone happy, they finished up and parted ways. The pizza people went out to survey their new acquisition and Jack headed in toward the city with a substantial cashier's check tucked in his wallet.

He'd been doing a little thinking while waiting to land. He hoped for enough time to pick up a gift for Gage. The first taxi in line had a woman driver. This was the first time he'd ever had a woman taxi driver in the States. "Michigan Avenue," was all he said as English never seemed to be a first language among taxi drivers. The less said, the less that could be misunderstood. He'd try to work in directions a step at a time. Actually, her English turned out to be pretty darn decent. She was from Jamaica and spoke with a charming calypso cadence. Like nearly every taxi driver in the world, she was supporting an entire extended family in a distant homeland. They talked all the way into the city. He'd spent some time in Kingston and had some good Jamaican friends. He kept in close contact with one of them, an official of the Airport Authority, and they'd gotten together a year or so ago down in Basseterre, on the island of St. Kitt's. That one little connecting thread of contact between two countries, or two cultures, or just two people made for an extremely pleasant ride in Chicago traffic and by the time they got near Michigan Avenue, she'd insisted that he look up half of her relatives on his next trip to Kingston.

"They'll treat you nice, mon," she insisted over and over in dialectical rhythm.

"See that jewelry store. Stop," he interrupted. "Can you pick me up in front of it in ten or fifteen minutes?" he asked as he paid the meter charge.

"Sure mon, sure. Fifteen minutes, I pick you up."

He had a feeling that he could count on her, so he'd better not let down on his end. He dashed into the posh shop in a real run for the gold. He went straight to a statuesque brunette with bangs cut dramatically across her forehead and hair so flattened that it looked like it had been ironed. He explained to her that he only had a few minutes, but he needed to buy something for a very special gal, one whose world revolved around art, and that he wanted something out of the ordinary to accompany the painting tucked under his arm.

The 'James Bond' salesgirl suggested something in an art-deco style. She steered him to a case that was more futuristic than deco looking. They were all beautiful, but there was something cold about them. "I think I'd like something with more warmth," he said looking up and down the long rows of lighted cases.

"Ah, she exclaimed, "I think you might like a piece of estate jewelry. We have the most exquisite diamond ring. It's from the estate of a Austrian countess and it's provenance is a real love story. It was purchased in the 30's by Count Stanislaw for his young bride, Sonia. During World War II she kept it pinned inside her corset, and although they lost everything else including all their art treasures, her ring stayed safe. She wore it until her death last summer and we purchased it at auction recently. We have all the paperwork on it, if you'd like to look at it."

Exquisite was the right word for it. The gold had a warm rich glow and the diamonds were clear and brilliant and spectacularly set. He'd never paid much attention to estate jewelry before, and he didn't know whether one could put much stock in the Count story, but the ring had Gage written all over it. "You've got a sale," he said hurriedly. "Can you size it, if it doesn't fit?"

"Yes sir," she replied reaching out to take his credit card. "Is this an engagement ring?"

He thought for a moment before answering, "I wouldn't be that presumptuous, no, it's just a gift."

"Lucky lady," sighed the clerk as Jack signed the American Express charge slip.

It took fourteen minutes to spend fourteen thousand dollars, he noted as he exited the front door carrying Countess Sonia's antique ring on to its next life cycle.

There she was, his Jamaican connection, waiting for him right in front of the store, blocking the outer traffic lane and waving those behind her around with big sweeping circles of her left hand. He ran to the taxi, hopped into the back seat and they shot forward into the beginning of rush hour traffic.

"Thanks for coming back. Don't kill us or anything, but I am in a little bit of a hurry. Can you get me to the Metropolitan Gallery pretty quickly? It's getting close to closing time and I've got a date with destiny."

"Yes, mon, if that's where you want to go," she affirmed. Then she looked into the rear view mirror making sure to catch his eye, "But, if you like, I can take you somewhere, you feel real good."

Holy shit! Propositioned by a Jamaican prostitute in Chicago, "I've got to get to the Gallery, I've got a deadline." Best not to show any reaction, after all, she was literally in the driver's seat and he didn't want to go the Gallery by way of Minnesota.

She didn't talk much after that, he didn't know if she was pouting or trying to concentrate on getting him there. She was driving at a pretty fast clip, not reckless, but faster than the speed limit when another taxi ran a stop sign and almost broadsided them. Jamaica slammed on her brakes and in the most bizarre happening of the day, her hair moved. And not with her head, her hair moved sideways. Her hair was, undoubtedly, a wig. Her long arm reached up to straighten the hair, and suddenly the light bulb went on. Jamaica wasn't a female prostitute. Jamaica wasn't a female at all. The craziest scenarios raced through his startled mind. If she is a he, is he a transvestite or a pimp, or a transvestite pimp?

It's a nutty world outside that cocoon of an airplane, he thought as he weighed the sequence of events. But, hey, the he or she or whatever was moving them right along toward the Gallery and that was all that mattered at the moment. He maintained a steady flow of conversation with the driver after the hair happening just to keep from changing the tempo of disposition in the taxi. It was four forty-five as they pulled up to the stately Metropolitan with its exterior clad in colorful contemporary banners. No doubt here, that there was an exhibit opening tomorrow. It was advertised flying in the wind at least fifty times.

He settled up with Jamaica, included ample gratuity, grabbed the kraft paper wrapped package that he'd been carrying from the moment he stepped out of the plane and bounded up the steps to a world which had opened up so unexpectedly, a world with a lot more permanence than any world that he'd been a part of in a very long time. She'd been on his mind all week.... in St. Louis, in Wyoming, and throughout the flight to Chicago. In fact, he found himself reveling in the premise that she was such an important element of his life. He clutched his pocket for the ring box and reassured of the presence of the tiny treasure, he hurried through the door as Nelson was buffing the brass handles for one last time this evening.

"Where will I find Gage McClendon?" he inquired of the doorman.

"She's still in the building, 'The Greatest Show On Earth' opens tomorrow."

"Wasn't that a movie?" Jack asked offhandedly.

"Yea," he smiled. "Do you know who was in it?"

"Let me think about it. First, I've got to catch Ms. McClendon before she leaves."

"She can't leave without coming by here, but her office is all the way down this corridor, at the end take a left and it's the first office on the left."

"Thanks, mate," Jack said hurrying off before he was caught in further movie trivia. The corridor floors seemed to have an aura of, be careful, we're ready for tomorrow. He walked lightly but quickly, following the doorman's directions straight to the office of the Exhibit Director. The office appeared empty. "Hello," he uttered through the stabbing angst of having missing her.

As Greta came back from the Gallery area, she encountered a handsome stranger standing at the door of the office. "Can I help you?" she asked.

"Hello. Yes, I'm looking for Gage."

"She's in the Gallery area somewhere, just wander down that way," she replied pointing in the direction of more banners and the entry to the major display areas.

He wasn't prepared for the impact of the show. The bold pieces were awesome and he got so caught up in the art experience that for a moment forgot his mission. He wandered slowly around the first room savoring the talent, the discipline, the style, and all the technical know how that elevates an artist to a major gallery. In aircraft jargon, the term 'Sunday pilot' is synonymous with 'the lesser lot' and transposed to the art arena, he was himself definitely a lessor lot, a Sunday painter. He focused both on looking for Gage and enjoying a synoptic look at the very handsome and extremely professional exhibit.

He couldn't remember a time when he wasn't fascinated by art, just as he couldn't remember ever thinking of not flying for a living, both were strong drives. Flying suited his skills more, but art was a compelling Callahan passion. He observed and absorbed all he could in this bit of cursory reconnaissance.

He walked toward a side exhibit room and stopped. Suddenly, it was as if his heart clinched into a giant knot and pounded on the chest wall in a temper tantrum. She was there, not alone, and it was definitely not the scene that had played over and over in his mind on the flight into Chicago. The two were standing in the center of the room, not in just a little squeeze or little hug, but with arms locked around each other in a bold sweeping embrace. Jack waited silently for a couple of minutes but they never made an attempt to part. A dark haired, handsome guy and the gal who occupied almost all the flyer's waking moments seemed to have all they needed inside this embrace.

He couldn't move, didn't move, waiting for a trick of the eye to play out. But it didn't play out, it lingered, and he encountered a brief sensation of drowning in the waves of nausea that washed over him.

He turned away and they were never aware of his presence. The walk back down the corridor was as quick as the walk in, but this time it was with heavy steps not the light hearted pace that had carried him into the Gallery. The only break from the heavy cadence of his footsteps was the moment that it took to lay his card in a fish bowl of cards on a desk. The doorman was getting ready to leave but he waited to ask if he'd found Ms. McClendon.

"Yes, I did, thanks," was the extent of Jack's response. He proceeded down the steps and hailed a taxi. Where do pilots go when the world gets rotten? Up, of course, so he headed to the airport. He had to be back in Jakarta in a few days anyway. The cab driver was a non-communicative Algerian. It was just as well, he needed the quiet. It was not supposed to be this way. What did he miss? He was usually better at reading people. "Forget it," he rebuked himself, "you've got a long trip ahead."

The radio in the cab was playing "I Will Always Love You" from the movie "The Bodyguard", and for a second he was Kevin Costner standing alongside the plane on the tarmac. It was a bit of a struggle to keep his emotions in check. Gage should have been the one. True, he'd never asked about her life in Chicago… hindsight, never assume anything!

Midway Airport was coming up on the horizon. He'd need to collect his flight bag. He was still carrying his offerings to Gage, the brown paper wrapped package and the love story estate ring. There was shuttle service to O'Hara and straight through International Customs.

16

Frank folded the tripod and Gage placed the lenses back in their cloth covers. They placed the equipment on a bench in the middle of the room and Frank turned to say , "Well done." It was then he saw the tears streaming down her eyes and dripping from her nose. He'd noted she seemed fragile earlier, and saw an unusually quiet demeanor, but he hadn't picked up on the depth of her emotions. He didn't say anything, just wrapped his arms around her and held her gently. She didn't make a sound, the tears were silent but seemingly endless. He stroked the back of her head and waited. After four or five minutes, when she'd purged an entire two years of tears, she looked at Frank with swollen eyes and mascara tracks on blistery red cheeks and thanked her good friend for his always there for you support. He took her chin in his hand and kissed both of her fiery bloated eyelids.

"I knew this was coming, I could feel everything beginning to collide at one time," she confessed. "It's crazy, but I feel such despair that Mac couldn't see this exhibit. I suppose, I also feel guilty that he had to die and I get to go on living, when his paintings clearly show how much he cherished life and its day to day challenges."

"Honey, it's normal for you to feel sad, but don't let the guilt factor pull you down. Are you also feeling guilty about last weekend?"

Gage looked him straight in the eye and answered, "Strangely enough, I don't."

"I'm glad of that, because you have nothing to feel guilty over. Some explaining, maybe, but that's to me. Come on, let's get out of here, it's my turn to buy dinner, that is, if you've got any make-up in your office. You could do with a little repair, otherwise, we're going to a fast food drive thru."

That gave her a quick reality check, and she even managed a chuckle. You might be dying but if you were with Frank, he would insist that your looking elegant in your demise. Himself, he would no doubt insist on a tanning session as part of his last rites.

They gathered the equipment from the bench and started slowly back to her office. Frank turned back for one more glance. "What a tribute," he remarked.

As they walked, Gage said softly, "Yes it is. I think I finally said goodbye to Mac."

Greta met them in the hall, "Is there anything else that we need to do this evening? Whoa, are you okay?... the exhibit, huh?"

"Yea, but I'm fine now. Frank won't take me to dinner like this though, so I've got to clean up. As far as I know, we're finished. Go check on your kids. Hear anything from Mike?"

"Where's Mike?" Frank questioned.

"Don't ask, that is if you don't want another dose of tears," Gage answered. "See you in the morning, Gret."

Greta hurried off and as soon as she got out of earshot, he asked again about Mike. He too, was stunned that they were separated. Mike was in the office occasionally waiting on Greta when Frank was there to see Gage and there was always lively conversation being bantered about. They seemed genuinely compatible. "Well, that reinforces my staying single. If they can't make it work, I sure as hell couldn't."

"It's been a real bummer for her and the kids," Gage informed him. The make-up repair was taking a little longer than just a touch-up. It needed to start from scratch. Frank was patient and kind enough to let her know that the results were worth the wait. She felt light and happy, as though tears had exorcized the demons... real or imaginary.

On this walk toward the front door, there was a decidedly different tempo, a light and almost reckless feeling. The doorman was gone, but had he have been there he would have seen Gene Kelly and Leslie Caron hand in hand down the Gallery steps in a comical rendition of the famous duo's classic dance moves.

They had a big discussion on where to go to eat. Frank won, he always won when it came to food. He'd probably tried every ethnic food establishment in Chicago, food was an experience, a happening. This time he won on Greek cuisine. They headed to the Athenia in separate vehicles, Gage didn't want to be out too late and Frank had a hard time leaving once he got into good food and good booze.

Why wasn't she surprised that the host knew him by name. "Frankie, Frankie," he called out pumping Frank's hand up and down repeatedly. "Got just the spot for you and the pretty lady, a quiet little corner."

"Thanks, Nick."

He seated them and rattled off the specials so quickly in his heavy accent that Gage looked at Frank with an expression of complete blankness. "You order for me," she requested.

"I always have Dolmades, when I come here."

"And, what is it?"

"It's grape leaves stuffed with lamb and rice and mint with avgolemono sauce, the best in Chicago. But you don't like lamb, so let's order it with beef for you. Sound okay?"

"Sounds great. I'm starved."

They ordered drinks and settled in for a pleasant wait on their meal. "Okay, ready to tell me about last weekend?" Frank prompted.

"It was just last week, wasn't it? God, it seems like a month, I've been so busy since I got back." She took her drink from the waiter and began her story. "Okay, I was sitting in a restaurant down on the riverbank in Cape Girardeau last Wednesday night visiting with a little group of arty people who live in the vicinity, when this prince, this Greek god, this super handsome guy... ."

"Enough slobbering," he interrupted, "I get the picture."

"His name is Jack Callahan. You'd like him, he was Viet Nam, too. Major JC Callahan was a cool pilot flying dangerous missions in a make-do refitted plane. Cavalier, maybe that's the best term for those guys. Anyway, I knew him from there. Nothing between us, he was married and I was engaged to Mac. He was in Chicago Wednesday to sell an airplane and saw my name in a flyer on the exhibit. My name isn't exactly common, so it caught his attention and he remembered that I was coming back from Nam to marry an artist. He read the synopsis about the late artist, and then he called my office and Greta, bless her little aching heart, told him where I was."

She went on talking about that fateful evening in great detail, telling of making plans to meet Saturday evening after he got back from a trip to Atlanta. She even told Frank that when Jack asked if he could bring anything or do anything for her, she had answered, just touch me.

"Doesn't sound like you," Frank pondered aloud. "You're not typically that forward, I mean that seems out of character. By the way, is he still married?"

"No, silly."

"Well, I heard you say, he was married"

"Was, Frank, was married, emphasis on was."

"Alright, alright, cool down."

"Okay, I apologize. I've got lots to confess, plus a lot that I won't, however, I bought a red dress Saturday afternoon, a soft red crepe, and I have a fairly decent tan so I think I looked passable for an old broad. We met in a town about seventy miles north of Cape. The town in itself is romantic and historic with an old world French background.

And the food, oh yes, a meal you'd have loved. The swordfish was a delicacy, brought in fresh, and really splendid"

"I can bet you weren't thinking that poor old Frank was missing a super meal, right?"

She grinned, "I admit it, you were absolutely nowhere in my thoughts."

" Don't sound so smug."

"But Frank, this is the kicker. For that entire evening, in a way, we owned the bar. The people in the bar were our party. Jack bought rounds of drinks and we gave toasts and we danced.... god, did we dance. Then this great big bike rider looking guy lifted me up on the bar and had the band play Patsy Kline's 'Crazy'. And we melded into the most sensual slow dance that you can imagine... we weren't like exhibitionists for the bar people, we were two people lost to everything in the world except each other."

"I'm impressed, I'm jealous, and I'm envious all in one. But you know what, I'm happy for you. Go on."

She spoke a little more guardedly as she told him about the hotel, not quite sure where good taste ended in talking about intimacy that involved another man. She described the old hotel, its front desk and the clerk, then worked her way slowly to the ceiling fan with a red dress trailing like a kite streamer. "When you're with someone who has only to look at you and bring you to melting temperature at dinner, imagine if you can, later on in the evening a darkened bar, a pretty decent dance band and the energy flow of two bodies moving to the beat of provocative night sounds. And Frank, from there it only gets better. It was a night so totally spontaneous, maybe that's what made it work."

"I can't wait to meet the guy who walked right through the invisible wall that you built around yourself. He didn't have to dismantle it a little at a time, he just walked right through it. One hell of a feat, does he have any idea how unapproachable you've been?"

"Probably not, but this was different."

"Alright, help me out, from a man's point of total frustration at not being able to figure women out, tell me what made it different?"

She thought for a moment, "Everything was right. He's attractive, compassionate, intelligent, and articulate. And could be that I was drawing from romanticized war memories, the intrigue of those living on the edge, pushing their fates to the limits. Was that enough to make it different? I really don't know. I suspect that even the food was part of it, that the music set a mood, the old hotel....all of it, the chemistry was right, and that's all I know."

"You've got something special there girl, don't lose it. In all my life and all my amours, I can't say that I ever came close to where you've just been. When am I going to get to meet Mr. Perfect?"

"I'm certain he'll be here tomorrow, he said he'd be here for the opening. Speaking of openings, I'd better be going. I've got girl things to do before tomorrow, fingernails, hair color... ."

"Stop, don't destroy the myth. I like to think that you babes walk around just naturally beautiful. Come on, I'll walk you to your car."

17

He collected his flight bag from the locker and boarded the shuttle bus for O'Hara. Pilots learn early on to sleep in small doses. Crazy schedules, time changes, nothing was routine, so it was a given that as soon as a pilot exited a cockpit, a cat nap wouldn't be long off. Normally, on a transfer trip like this, he would have been asleep before the shuttle bus filled with passengers. Not this time, he heard conversations that he didn't really want to hear, saw pierced eyebrows, navels, and tongues that he really didn't care to see and listened to cranky spats between kids and parents. It was dark now and he tried to focus outside the bus, the city lights brought a certain magic that is Chicago. Eventually, they reached their destination and he began to relax in the familiar environs of jet engines and flight calls.

He made his way to a bank of computer hook-ups and pulled a lap top out of the flight bag. Going on line, he entered his travel needs and worked out reservations for J. Callahan from Chicago to Jakarta, Indonesia. It was much faster than standing in long lines between rows of chrome stanchions. He pressed in credit card numbers, got confirmation and looked for a place to kill a three hour wait.

The pay phones had the symbolic look of hookers... teasing... call her... call her. He resisted. He walked right past them into the nearest V.I.P. lounge and then he walked right back out. He relented and he called. He didn't have her home number, he had her cell phone number but it apparently wasn't turned on. The Chicago phone book was loaded with names starting with Mc's so he went carefully down the pages, not knowing how it would be listed or even whether it would be listed. His finger stopped at G. McClendon. An initial used in a listing usually meant it was a woman, especially as there was no address listed. He dialed but hesitated at the last digit. Finally, gingerly punching in the last number, he waited... six, seven, eight rings and no answer.

In the lounge, a lively poker game was the happening event. Jack sat down near the players and became intrigued with some of the most amateurish poker plays he'd ever seen. If loud counted for something, they were having a grand time even though they spent most of their time talking about frozen pork bellies and corn futures. He figured them to be low level commodities traders. After a while poker and pork bellies got a little old, and he moved to a quieter area. He picked up the Wall Street Journal and read an article on economic indicators but was mindful that he wasn't absorbing anything he was reading so he gathered up the parcel and the flight bag and headed toward his gate. There he waited, watching aircraft take off and land as he'd done hundreds of times in airports all over the world. He even challenged himself to a mental count of the various airports, but quickly conceded that he himself was mentally challenged right now.

Los Angeles finally came up on the board and it wasn't long before they were loading. He was cutting it pretty close to get to Korean Air and go through customs for the 12:30 a.m. flight to Seoul. But he knew a lot of shortcuts around LAX and felt comfortable with the schedule. It was the five hour lay over in Seoul that he dreaded. Not that he dreaded Seoul itself, he hadn't spent much time there, and the brief excursions he had made into the city were always enjoyable. It was the five hour layover that was disturbing… five long hours to think about what might have been. He'd never been one to anticipate problems and here he was thinking in negatives. "Buddy, you've got it bad, and that ain't good," he said aloud to no one in particular.

He took his seat, chatted a bit with the hostess and ordered a drink. Booking last minute flights was usually easy in business class and he always had enough air miles for upgrades. As soon as the 747 reached altitude and leveled out, the hostess brought his scotch and water and he settled into a pleasant conversation with a Stanford professor, who it turned out had flown RF-102's in Viet Nam. In a time frame coincidence, the professor flew reconnaissance missions out of Tan Son Nhut killin' em with film about the same time the Dragon man was making his night time raids down south. Funny, how that long ago war was suddenly surfacing in his life right now. The two talked about legendary exploits of cracker jack aces and Montagnards and 'gotcha vines' and the role of the news media and then the horrendous sight of rows and rows of body bags on the tarmac. The body bags remembrances put a damper on the conversation and they sort of drifted to an end of the war stories and Jack fell into a sound sleep. Nevertheless, he couldn't get her out of his thoughts, the last recall of his conscious mind was, "With her, it should have been different."

Meanwhile the woman with whom it should have been different was on her way home from dinner and looking forward to tomorrow's opening. She couldn't bring herself to say it out loud, but she was eager to look beyond the opening. The anticipation of seeing him again was paramount to all else. Over and over, every conceivable combination of his name… Jack, JC, Jackson Calhoun, Major Callahan… she recited them rosary fashion. Then she'd laugh at herself and this throw back to high school behavior.

She opened the door and stood waiting for Pancho to begin his will beg for food act. He didn't appear and Gage felt a surge of dread as she began looking for him. Pancho Sanchez was in his favorite chair but was not moving, and her worst fear for her dear old cat had become reality. He had succumbed to old age. He was either fifteen or sixteen and she knew he couldn't have much time left. Her heart was pounding and her eyes filled with tears for the second time today. She quickly dialed Mrs. Giovanni's number and asked her to come over. There was something about death, even a cat's death, that she just didn't want to face alone.

Her neighbor's presence gave her the push to make arrangements for disposal. Mrs. Giovanni helped find a box. They put the furry little body in the furnace room and her neighbor offered to be available to let the pet crematorium people into the place tomorrow. Gage left her address and other pertinent information on the pet people's answering machine and she gave Mrs. Giovanni a signed check.

She then poured her neighbor a glass of wine. She couldn't find anything Italian, in fact everything in the wine rack was either California or Australian. But it didn't matter, neither one really wanted the drink, it just made the visit a little more sociable. Gage was restless, one minute she was sitting and the next minute she was pacing. They finally decided that they'd said all the comforting platitudes that they could think of, so it was okay to call it a night. She gave Mrs. Giovanni her deep-felt thanks and a big hug and walked along with her to her apartment.

Gage returned to her apartment and began those night before the show tasks that forever remain night before the show tasks like making sure that you have a new or clean suit, a power suit as it's called, and that your hair color is fresh and bright, little necessary aggravations of life.

As she walked past the telephone in the kitchen, she checked the caller ID, a lot of piddly calls, insurance agent, several friends, an auto club, and the usual unknown name, unknown numbers. Nothing identifiable interested her at the moment, she just wanted to immerse her fatigued body in a big fat tub of perfumed bubbles. She hurriedly did the hair color and nails, checked on the navy suit then ran the bath water. A scent of spice and sandalwood effused the air... first diluting the vexations of the day and then dissolving them as well as soothing those thoughts that begin to plague a woman in her fifties… a slight belly that no gym can push back into flat territory, eyelids not as taunt as they once were, and that cursed upper arm of swinging flesh. Funny, how a little session in pampered waters worked such wicked magic that she could once again become the woman that she wanted to see in the mirror. A woman balancing confidence and sensuality and looking fit and trim, "Now come on," she says, "you really are fit and trim." Maybe women take baths to talk to themselves. Men never take baths, that is unless there's a woman in the tub. Men take long showers, but do they talk to themselves, Gage wondered? She fantasized in the effervescence of the scented waters at her perception of a man talking in the shower… talking by checking his physique, all angles, and flexing his biceps thinking back to the body of a twenty year old… when he could pee faster and stay hard longer. Yep, she suspected that men talked to the mirror even before they ever got to the shower. What about the Major? He was lean and firm and "Wow," she blurted out, thinking about him, all six foot one inch of him stark naked in front of a mirror. "Oh yes, women do talk to themselves in their baths, men have no idea… ."

She slept well, surprisingly so, without pudgy old Pancho snugged up to her rib cage. She remembered running her hand along her side during the night just to check, knowing but still checking.

The morning light didn't beat her by much, she was always up early for an exhibit opening. It didn't open until ten o'clock but there was always something that needed last minute attention. There were a few details that she didn't think she'd spent enough time on, one being the music. She was taking someone else's word that this group was right for this show, she'd never heard them play at all and it really wasn't like her to not check further. They looked right, she rationalized.

18

The crowds were there. It looked like all of Chicago waiting outside the brass doors. Nelson looked highly official talking with his crew of ushers who would be working alongside gallery security. Once again there was the highly charged atmosphere that always precedes the moments before the doors swing open. The musicians were in place and had finished tuning. In fact they were playing some new age music that sounded quite appropriate. No need to have worried about their skills, they were a highly accomplished little group.

Ten o'clock arrived and the Gallery was ready to play host to the art lovers, and the curious, and the school classes, and the tourists, and they were all now spilling into the rooms and their chatter played in counterpoint to the music of the new age musicians. This was fun. This was what made the art world come alive. Every exhibit breathed new life into the canvases because each visitor brought with him or her a unique and personal interpretation of the paintings. These fresh perspectives were invaluable to keeping the paintings connected to future generations.

If a heart could truly rejoice, hers was now. She strolled in a detached sort of way around the rooms and heard wonderful compliments, not a negative remark anywhere. One of the most interesting comments was an old gentleman's reaction to the corporate board meeting inside the stomach painting. He might have interpreted it right. He told his companion that those board guys were probably ulcers in black suits. Gage was stunned, "Why didn't I think of that?" Once again, that was the marvel of these exhibits and she reveled in an ambience of sensory explosions.

She spent a lot of time during the day watching the doors, hoping to spot Jack so he wouldn't have to wind his way through this maze of humanity to find her. She saw Frank coming in to check the crowds. "Frank, over here," she called out waving through a school tour group.

"Great swarm, looks and sounds like a bee hive. And just how is Miss Queen Bee doing today?" he changed the light tone of his voice to one of concern.

"I'm okay. Well, actually, I'm relieved. It's always a relief to get to this point."

He looked around. "Is he here yet?"

"Who?" she returned without really thinking about what he'd said.

"Your hero, the guy who makes you slobber all over your adjectives."

" Oh... no, he isn't here yet," she replied, wishing she could have said yes, he's here.

"Shucks, how can I give my approval?"

"Sure, like I need your approval," Gage put her hands on her hips in mock protest. She was ready to show off her pilot friend, that was a major turnabout for her. Even so, she didn't like the fact that she was beginning to feel a little uneasy. He did say he'd be there for the opening and she had no reason to doubt his word. What if something had happened to him? No one would know to notify her. Shake it, that's silly, she scolded herself. He's been flying since he was sixteen, chances of something happening to him now at this particular time are remote, just plain remote. He'll be here. She busied herself answering questions. Some were rather profound questions, such as what was the deciding factor that let Mac feel secure enough early on to think that he would be able to support himself through art. She tried as best she could to be honest in her answers, however, there were some questions for which she simply had no answers.

Frank didn't hang around long. He congratulated her once again on a superb show and left shouting, "Call me when he comes in."

She smiled. She wouldn't tell Frank that she'd told Jack about him and mentioned that she'd like for him to meet Frank. His answer had been a humorous but polite, "I don't want to meet your god damn friend!"

The first day was a huge success in numbers and enthusiasm. Enthusiasm was always a rated factor almost equal to attendance numbers, so at this point Gage McClendon, Special Exhibit Director had done her job very well even though a shadowy feeling of restlessness hung over her personally. Nevertheless, the day went by swiftly. A normal opening day would have found a few of the staff going out after closing to celebrate a winner, but this time Gage hung around long past closing, talking to those who had to stay after the crowds were gone, the janitors and security. Along the same line, Greta was too caught up in her own problems to think about celebrating anything and Gage didn't want to celebrate without her. Reluctantly, she turned off the lights in her office and tried not to analyze that which she did not know.

It was a long commute home this trip. The mind didn't turn off on command, in fact it seemed to work overtime on worry mode. She pulled into the parking garage and walked to her apartment giving in to a very head down manner of carriage only to be startled erect at Mrs. Giovanni's shrill greeting, "honey, guess what, I've got good news for you."

Gage said facetiously, "not unless you're involved in a covert operation of hiding a guy in my apartment."

"Huh?" was the reaction followed by, "The pet people only charged you thirty five dollars, you know, we thought it would be at least sixty."

"Oh that's great, Mrs. Giovanni," she tried to sound upbeat. It wasn't the little Italian lady's fault that she felt churlish. She thanked her several times for helping out, but sidestepped inviting the lady inside this evening. Her enthusiasm was bridled in anxiety and she needed to get herself centered again. But with all the emotional preparations, Friday turned out to be a rerun of Thursday's anxieties. Even unlocking her apartment door was a wearying endeavor.

She closed the door, kicked off her shoes and wandered around the apartment aimlessly. She checked the phone calls... still hoping, and decided to turn in early. Saturday was always the zenith in attendance. At this point, she was thankful that she didn't have to be there on Sunday.

Seven hours into a sound sleep, her inner time mechanism jangled her back to a state of consciousness and she moved quickly to get on with the day. No matter what, she loved the crowds and loved seeing people genuinely bond with works of art. Although, this day carried much more intensity for her because she needed desperately to connect last weekend with today.

It was entirely too warm for coffee, so she hurried into Anzio's, ordered an iced mocha to go and was still the first of the staff to show up on this sultry Saturday morning. If she immersed herself in the workings of the day, then there wouldn't be time to fret and sometime today things would work out the way they were supposed to... surely!

"Morning, Gret," she called out to her friend as she came into the office.

"Hi," Greta responded. "I'm bushed and we haven't even gotten into the day. Thank heavens, we don't have to come in every Saturday. I had a heck of a time getting the boys parceled out for rides to their soccer games. I called Mike, but he had fifty eleven flimsy excuses why he couldn't drive them. I think the son of a bitch had the other woman in his apartment. Oh hell, Gage, I've got to get past this, it's driving me crazy."

"Don't let it, if you do, he wins."

Yeah, you're right, you wanna do something tonight?"

Gage thought for a moment, she still hadn't said anything to Greta about last weekend. "I don't know, let's see how the day goes." It was time to open the Gallery and get immersed in the crowd, the process which she hoped was going to help her pass time. "I'll be out on the floor, in case anyone is looking for me."

The crowds stayed steady all day. At one point, she looked across the room and saw Elliott. He was standing very still, watching her intently and she suddenly wanted to disappear. She tried not to make eye contact so she could hurry away without being obvious that she was avoiding him. She was on the wrong side of the building to go anywhere other than into the next exhibit room, but that was okay, because there were even more people in that area and maybe she could somehow play cat and mouse around the rooms until she lost him. She couldn't quite bring herself to believe that her old friend was beginning to frighten her, but every time he came into the picture she felt nauseous and uncomfortable. She visited with some out of towners and answered a few questions for a elderly couple and got over the momentary queasiness. She hung around the main area for awhile and then made a break to go back to the office.

"Avoiding me?" Elliot stepped out in front of her from a recess in the corridor.

His sudden appearance jolted her so violently that the blood rushed from her head and she felt her knees begin to buckle. He reached out to steady her. "Sorry, didn't mean to scare you," he apologized. "Let's go get something to drink and let you sit down a moment."

"Elliott, I can't. I'm working." He seemed so sincere she felt a little guilty at thinking of him as some kind of stalker.

"Then I'll pick you up after work," he pressed close enough that she could feel his breath in her face.

She had a feeling her next words weren't going to set well with him, "Greta is having some problems and I've promised to go out with her this evening."

Gage couldn't read his reaction. He didn't say anything. He saluted and walked slowly down the corridor then turned around and waved. She rubbed her arms. They were covered with goosebumps and she was shivering. She headed to her office to get something to head off what was suddenly becoming a major headache.

Greta was rummaging through their medicine stash as she walked into the office. "You too?" Gage asked. "Give me a couple, of anything, please. You're right, Elliott is spooky. Just now he jumped out at me in the hall, real weird like."

"Honey, stay away from that guy. I can tell you he's trouble. Of course, right now I wish a pox on all testosterone glands, my sons and father excluded."

They laughed. Gage took the headache pills and ate a couple of crackers with cream cheese. It was long past lunch time and she thought perhaps the source of her angst might be hunger. A basket of fruit had been delivered to their office this morning so she helped herself to a tangerine. Mr. Espinosa called her to give a group of Japanese tourists a personal tour of the exhibit and she spent the next two hours explaining and bowing. She got caught up in the bowing gesture to be polite, but backed off when she realized that she was beginning to initiate the ritual.

The day was beginning to wind down and she hadn't gotten the visit that she'd so anticipated. She was beginning to wilt in spirit and wasn't sure that she wanted to go out with Greta and listen to further depressing conversation. It was a chore to walk back to the office where Greta was turning off the computers. "Gage, are you okay? I get the feeling that there's something going on with you, but I can't put my finger on just what it is. If there was a man in your life, I'd guess that you have man problems. There's not a guy, is there?"

Gage sat down on the corner of the desk. She might as well confide in Greta, maybe it would help her to look beyond her own problems. "I'm a little down, Gret. A friend, a guy friend, was supposed to come to Chicago to see me and the exhibit this week and the week is just about gone and he didn't show."

"Someone special?"

" I thought so."

"Well, the only man who showed up here today for you was that creep Elliott, and I'm sure as hell glad that he's not Mr. Special. What about the guy who was here Wednesday?"

"Frank? Are you kidding? Well, he probably is Mr. Special to his beautiful bevy of cover girls."

"No, I didn't mean him. That handsome dude who went in the Gallery looking for you when you were working with Frank on the photos."

"No one came in the Gallery." Gage straightened up and got up from the desk, "What time, Greta?"

"Oh, I don't know, probably about four thirty or quarter to five. I was getting ready to leave when he popped his head in the door and asked for you. I gave him directions and told him you were just finishing up. He was carrying something wrapped in kraft paper, looked like it could have been a painting so I assumed he was an artist looking for a show."

"Greta, please, carefully.... describe him."

"Sheesh! I only saw him for a minute at the most. Since I'm not into positive declarations about men right now, it's a little difficult for me to admit that he was handsome. Okay, let me think... he had light eyes, a great head of hair, sunbleached or maybe with some gray... oh, and a kind smile. Couldn't tell how old he was. "

" Quickly, what kind of clothes?" Her heart was racing now.

" I don't know. I was tired and thinking about supper. Maybe tan or gray, oh he had those little tabs on his shirt on the shoulders, like a safari shirt."

"Epaulettes?"

"I don't know what they're called."

All of a sudden, Gage felt such internal pressure that she thought her head was going to explode. She pounded her fists on the desk and in a repetitive mantra-like sequence repeated over and over, "No... no... no... no!"

"Get hold of yourself, it's not as bad as it seems. I think I remember seeing him put his card in the fish bowl." The fish bowl wasn't an aquarium, it was more like a brandy snifter where all the sales reps or any other visitor left their business cards. It wouldn't be the first time they'd found a crucial address in their fishbowl. Greta scurried across the room and quickly retrieved a beige card from the top of the pile. "See, here it is, you can call him."

She grabbed the card. It was him!... JC Callahan, Contract Flying, International. Scribbled in smudged pencil was a phone number. It was a long number that began with an 011, so she knew it was an international number, but she had no idea whether it was a current number or even whether it was his at all. The way it was written, sort of cock-eyed on the card, it could have been a number that someone else had written to give him. She was devastated and Greta had now become the counselor. Gage felt paralyzed, she couldn't move. All she could do was stare at the card and wonder what went wrong... what went so terribly wrong. It wasn't something simple like Greta imagined that could be fixed with a phone call. Jack was more than likely a world away by now... literally on the other side of the world. How can you fix anything with a person whose lifestyle is so global that just locating him could be an impossibility, not overlooking the fact that he might choose to have you not find him. "Look honey, if he wanted to see you, why didn't he wait a few minutes until you were finished with the photos?"

Gage didn't answer for the longest time and when she did, it was in a very quiet tone of voice, "I know now. I know. When Frank and I finished with the photos, I was emotional. I was, in a way, saying goodbye to Mac. I knew it was time to get on with my life, and I was struggling to keep myself intact and then, I just lost it." She was talking barely above a whisper now, "the floodgates opened and every emotion that I should have let out sooner came pouring out all at once. Frank put his arms around me and held me tightly for a few minutes, neither one of us saying much. He let me get it all out of my system." After that she was silent, hesitating to put into words the fact that her catharsis, which was meant to move her into a new life cycle, was probably the killer of her new life cycle.

Greta guessed the rest. "And this guy saw Frank with his arms around you, right?"

"Probably so... yes. We finished up about four forty five. Oh, Greta... god, I can't believe it. I haven't had a chance to tell you about last weekend, but this guy is someone from somewhere long ago and last weekend was so wonderful, and it's destroyed now. It's all gone!" She pressed on her abdomen, realizing what it meant to have a deep down gut ache. And maybe it wasn't the medical definition of a heart attack, but her heart really did ache.

Greta took her hand, "Come on we're going to dinner and figure this thing out."

Gage looked in the mirror and Frank's remarks last night about taking her to a fast food drive thru because of her disarray came back to her again this evening. Same scenario, moreover, Frank would probably, as he loved to do, make a big deal of it and threaten to get the fashion police after her. She agreed to go to dinner and while Greta checked with the sitter, Gage rearranged her face and tried to rearrange her disposition. "Gret, what if we pick up some Chinese and go back to my apartment? I've got wine."

"Got any beer? I don't like wine."

"No, but we can stop and get some. Come on."

Greta decided to pick up the beer, so she could choose the brand and Gage headed to a hole in the wall Chinese take out place near her apartment. Both overbought, they could have sustained for a fortnight with their provisos. They arrived at the apartment almost simultaneously, both had to laugh at their party for two buying for twelve mentality. They rationalized that they could indeed eat everything they'd bought, and then they tried, all evening.

Gage was anxious to get back to everything that Greta could remember about Jack. She wanted to know about his mood, more about the package he carried, and whether she ever saw him again after he left their office.

"Slow down," Greta moaned. She opened a beer, "I suppose, you could say he seemed happy, he was smiling when he asked for you."

"What about the package? You're pretty sure it was a painting?"

"Pretty sure, it was about twenty by twenty four inches. It was wrapped in brown paper, old brown paper."

"That had to be one of his paintings. He was going to show me something he did in Vietnam. Greta, how could we come so close and then lose it so quickly?"

"Well, I don't know, but then there are pieces of this puzzle that I seem to be in the dark about. Who is this guy and how did he get to be a major player in your life all of a sudden?" She asked a lot more questions in rapid fire succession until Gage finally stopped her.

"Okay, let me go back to my trip to Cape. Well, first let me go back to the airport here. He was in Chicago to sell a plane and happened to see a flyer on the exhibit... recognized my name... talked to you... yes you... on the phone and you told him where I was."

"Oh, I remember that."

"Then he flew to Cape and actually found me in a restaurant last Thursday night."

Greta was following the story intently. "But how did you know each other in the first place?"

"We were in Vietnam at the same time. He was a pilot and I worked at the USO. And to make a long story short, we met again last Saturday night and had the most wonderful fairy tale evening and then spent the night together. There's a lot more, but I just haven't had time to just sit down with you and go through it."

"Go, girl!" she raised her bottle in a toast. " McClendon, when you do something, you do it big time! You really like the guy, don't you?"

"Like him? Lightning, strike me dead if I lie... I'm crazy about him."

Greta put her hands in the air, "No lightning... no thunderbolt... must be okay," she teased. "He found you, now we have to find him. Can't be that hard, it's just a little ole world out there."

"Greta, you're a silly goat... it's a great big world."

"I like my slant on it better. Got any idea, where he might be, Philadelphia, New York, Sacramento?"

"Jakarta, Indonesia, possibly."

"Oh hell," Greta's response was swift and succinct. "Well, in that case, maybe the world is a little bigger than my conception. But not to fear. If you think he's worth it, then I do too and we'll track him down." She opened another beer and called to check on the kids. The sitter asked if it was alright if she just spent the night there as her husband was out of town and she and the boys were settled in with a couple of good movies for the evening. Greta liked the idea because she really didn't want to leave Gage by herself until they had some kind of game plan for finding this guy. But lordy, Jakarta, Indonesia! She didn't even know if you went east or west to get to that part of the world. She grabbed an unopened container of pork fried rice to help her think.

Gage sat cross legged on the floor in front of the leather sofa. She had his card in her hand. "We could call this number, but it could be anybody's number anywhere in the world and I don't know what time it might be, wherever it is. And I don't know if he's had time to get back to Jakarta or wherever or whether he was going straight back. He did ask me to meet him in Singapore."

"When?"

"I really don't think he was going there from here. It was just something he said sort of matter of factly, like you'd say, can you meet me at the donut shop or something. Maybe Singapore is just a nice place to get away to sometime."

"Oh yeah, like we all say, can you meet me in Singapore... sure buddy, today or tomorrow," she said in mockery.

"There are a lot of vagaries to think about. What if he doesn't want me to contact him?"

Greta replied sharply, "Well, it's a sure thing that we won't know, if we don't try. Give me that number." She picked up the phone, then hesitated and handed it to Gage. "I don't know how to make an international call."

Gage carefully dialed the long sequence of numbers, fearful she'd wake some poor soul who couldn't understand an English apology. There was a benumbing silence after she finished the last number, she knew to expect a few seconds delay on some overseas calls, so she held the phone tightly smashed into her ear and then she heard it ring. It was a different ring than Chicago's. It was a deep, drawn-out ring, two times, three times... then , "Sheraton Bandara,"

"Do you have an American staying there, a Jack Callahan?" She tried to enunciate very carefully. Greta was sitting across the room with both hands in the air and her fingers crossed. A long pause, then a different voice came on the line. She repeated the same question again and the young female voice said, "Meestr Collahon, no today." Well, what did that mean? Did it mean that he just wasn't there today, or did it mean simply that there was no Meestr Collahon?

"Do you speak English?"

"Yes," was the reply but then the voice went away, although the line was still open. Once again, she waited.

"May I help you?" a decidedly Australian accent came on the line.

"Yes, please, I'm trying to contact Jack Callahan. Is he registered there and what country am I calling?"

"This is Jakarta, Indonesia and yes, Mr. Callahan is staying with us, but he has not picked up his messages for some time. There is no answer in his room. Wait just a moment." It grew quiet again and soon the Aussie accent came back, "there is a notation asking that we hold Mr. Callahan's messages and it does indicate that he was to be gone a couple of weeks. According to that, he should be back in the next couple of days."

"Oh thank you so very much, what is your name in case I need to get back in touch again?"

"My name is Mavis, is there anything else I can do for you?"

"Thanks so much Mavis, no, you've been a great help."

Greta uncrossed her fingers and started counting, "One... we know what country he will be in soon. Two... we know what hotel. Three... will simply be making the connection with him. I wish we'd have found out what time it was over there. It's gonna be a long wait. It's always long when you're waiting for something you want so badly. It's like the more you want it, the more you're afraid that just wanting it so badly will make it not happen."

She had to admit that it was just exactly as Greta laid it out. Gage wanted this to work out so badly that she was afraid that the desperation would jinx the outcome. They talked on and kept eating all evening, moving into the eggrolls at this point and fixing themselves a pot of green tea. It was getting too late for Greta to have any more alcohol and drive home.

"This will work out," Greta kept saying. "It's got to. The last couple of years have been so reclusive for you that it's good to see you get excited about a guy. If he only knew."

"He knew last week."

"He will again. How about this, I haven't mentioned Mike all evening. Your guy is good for me too. I've got to call it an evening and go home soon ....but one more time, let's call one more time tonight."

Gage was hesitant. It hadn't been two hours since their first attempt. But Greta was insistent, so they went through the whole sequence once more dialing the numbers, waiting for the phone to ring, then hearing "Sheraton Bandara" again. Asking and waiting once again , until a voice with the same inflection as before replied, "Meestr Collahon, no today." She had no idea what the costs were for phone calls to Jakarta, and maybe was better off not knowing at this point. Nevertheless, she decided that this was the last try tonight. Greta helped tidy up, it looked like a college dorm with food on the tables as well as the floor.

"Thanks for coming over Greta, thanks for just being here for me."

"Like you've not been there for me, gal. It works both ways. Cheer up, talk to you tomorrow." Gage walked to the car with her and they spent a few more minutes going over the whole scenario again.

She blocked tomorrow intentionally and concentrated on nothing. In the background, a mellow Keb Mo CD warned of "The Last Bad Deal Goin' Down".

19

The morning was gray and soggy. Rain was way overdue and this morning's design to dump all of the stored up rains on top of this downpour made for a virtual monsoon. Gage lingered in bed a little later than usual, partly because the darkness of the day tricked the body into a lengthier nocturnal mode, and partly to keep the telephone from being too convenient to her mission du jour. She finally decided to join Sunday morning with a stack of microwavable pancakes and a cup of Frank's gourmet coffee. He stockpiled his favorite brew everywhere he visited, it wouldn't do for Frank to suffer the embarrassment of supermarket coffee.

She dawdled. She carefully tore the barcode label off the front of a magazine, it wouldn't read any differently, but it'd look nicer. The plants got a Sunday morning watering and the newspapers were gathered together and tied for recycling. Mid morning found her still circling the phone with incidental tasks. For Gage, who was geared to concentrated productivity, this little 'circle the wagons' dance had to stop. She pulled from resources deep inside to bolster her in the attempt to square things up with the only man in the world who could put her in a situation of wanting to go through this uncertainty.

Her hand showed a slight tremor as she reread the penciled numbers and once again, even more slowly this time dialed the Jakarta phone number. Same slow ring, same dialectical inflection, "Sheraton Bandara".

"Please ring the room for Jack Callahan," she said very distinctly.

"Yes, please," was the reply.

Then the voice that she hoped to hear almost stopped her speechless, "Hello."

"Jack," was all she could get out.

"Gage?" he sounded stunned.

She couldn't tell if it was good stunned or just stunned, but at least she had him on the phone, albeit, on the other side of the world. It wasn't the way she'd have liked to have held this conversation, nevertheless, she was thankful for any contact at all. "Yes, it's me and please don't hang up, I've got some explaining to do."

"I'm not going to hang up, hey, it's good to hear from you."

"First of all," she stopped for a second and then blurted out, "is Singapore still an option?"

"Sure is. What's going on?"

"You are such a dear, and I miss you more than I've ever missed anyone in my life." The words poured out in a full flowing stream of excitement. " I waited anxiously all week only to have most odious twist of fate shatter... " She stopped, he was so quiet. "Are you still there?"

"Yes, I am... Gage, before you exasperate yourself, I still feel exactly as I did last week about you." He chuckled, " so take your time, I'm not going to vaporize, and if we get cut off, I promise to call you back."

"Thanks," she sighed and then began again. "Anyway, I found out that you did come to the exhibit. Unfortunately it was at the very time we were finishing up photographing. To make it short, I think that the stress of putting the exhibit together finally caught up with me and I was dealing with the reality of acknowledging that my life was moving on. It was an extremely emotional few minutes and Frank, who is my best friend and also our photographer, was caring enough to wrap his arms around me and stay with me until I got it out of my system."

Jack felt he had a little explaining to do also. "Coming back, I thought about whether or not I was justified in walking away without making contact with you. But you looked so comfortable."

"Comfortable, yes. More than that, no."

He spoke softly, "I came within twenty feet of you and didn't follow through. That's the real heart breaker. Girl, you don't have any idea how I've missed you. We found something special together and I damn sure don't want to lose it. Did I hear you correctly, did I really hear you ask, is Singapore an option? Would you repeat that one more time, please? " he asked incredulously.

"Is Singapore... still... an option?

"It sure as hell is, do you read me?"

"Loud and clear, Major."

"Shoot me a date and I'll work on it from this end," he offered.

The conversation was moving faster than her mind could assimilate the times zone changes and layovers so she threw out a day that seemed reasonably attainable. "What if I worked it out to arrive in Singapore Thursday afternoon, your time?"

"You work out the details, I guarantee I'll be there to meet you. It's a short trip from here to Singapore. You have a valid passport, right?"

" Yep, passport's okay. What airlines?"

"Singapore Airlines." He added, "I've got a food pallet to fly to one of the islands on Thursday morning but this will work. Wait a minute, hang up and let me call you back. Your phone bill is tooling along a high dollar track right now and I've got some cheap international phone cards."

"I know this sounds insecure, but I'm afraid to hang up. I'm afraid of losing you again."

He answered reassuringly, " The phone service is pretty good from here. Just sit tight, I'll call right back." He could sense the apprehension in her voice.

She hung up. There was a sense of uneasiness as the receiver clicked onto the cradle. She grabbed a glass of water to loosen up a dry throat, curled up in the big overstuffed chair and waited. The phone rang. It was beautiful, funny she'd never noticed the sweetness of its ringing before. "Hello," she answered cautiously.

"Jarkarta here," he called out. " That wasn't bad, was it? I've got a fistful of phone cards so let's start using them. You talk first. I just want to listen to your voice."

"Well... I miss you. It's a rainy Sunday morning here... but now there's you and suddenly there are rainbows. Is that okay?"

"Great for starters. Now from my end... you don't know it, but I'm looking at you, babe."

"Huh? Like paranormal something or other?"

"Not quite," he answered. He went on to tell her about the painting that he'd picked up at Pliny's, one that he'd painted in Viet Nam. A perfect likeness of the woman on the Chicago end of his telephone conversation.

She was astonished and thoroughly flattered. He'd painted her thirty years ago and he still had the painting. She'd never sat for it. She didn't know he painted at all until last week. "I can't wait to see it, although, I don't know if I want to see how much I've changed."

He glanced across the room where the painting rested against the wall. The old kraft paper wrapper had gotten torn on his trip back and he could see the very contemporary Gage McClendon looking wistful but vibrant. "Remember, I told you that I always painted everything the way I thought they or it would look in the future, well, the future is here. The painting looks exactly like you do today."

"You're kidding! Callahan, you're wonderment personified. I can't wait to see it... and I can't wait to see you."

He continued, "the night I walked into that restaurant in Cape and asked for you, the waitress pointed to a table where I saw the painting that I'd done thirty years ago. Only this painting was talking and laughing and very much alive. At that moment, I fell in love."

"You... you take my breath away."

"I'd like to take your breath away. I'd like to inhale every bit of breath from your body and feed it back to you slowly with love... and chocolates," he added jovially. "What in the name of that lady saint, are we doing half a world apart?"

They both lamented that this was one heck of a predicament. They talked through a one hour phone card and started on the second with the same themes over and over. From her end it was will there still be a Jack Callahan in my life when I wake up tomorrow, will there really be this special someone whose intensity brings the nirvana of perfect bliss? And from his side of the world... the overwhelming desire for her physical presence, her perfume, her tenderness.

They laughed. They joked. They were thoroughly comfortable in what they jokingly called phone sex. There were no off limits. Last week had pretty well taken care of that and with all barriers down, they were able to simply enjoy each other without reserve.

They talked about their backgrounds and the relationships to who they are today. Jack told Gage about growing up in Wyoming and how his sister stayed home to run the farm and all about her new friend, Curtiss Markhan with the Indian name of Raven Tall Wing. He talked about making practice landings in the pastures on the farm and theorized that a strong trait of restlessness lay behind his desire to fly.

She told him about dear old grandmother Bayswater and about her own parents, Mariette and Lachlan who didn't marry until they were in their forties. Gage was an only child and she remarked to Jack that she always felt that she had three grandparents instead of two parents and a grandparent. Her mother worked long hours as a clerk at Marshall Field's and her grandmother watched over her after school. Grandma Bayswater's house was full of art books and the many hours spent looking through the big colorful books probably predestined her toward a career in art. And because she had no artistic talent herself she looked toward the art history side of the field. She lost both parents and her grandmother while she was in college and concluded that maybe that was where she was coming from in her worry that Jack's entry in her life would be in a transient role.

Finally, from both sides of the world they sensed trivia beginning to drive the conversation and they decided that it was time to disconnect... at least for this day.

"It's damned dumb to have to say goodbye," Jack apologized. "But there's not a whole hell of a lot of choice. I'll call tomorrow evening to get your flight info. When's the best time to catch you at home?"

"I'll be here by six o'clock."

"I'll figure out the time changes and try you then. If I don't call right at six, don't be alarmed. It could mean I'm out in the field and that I'm not in a position where I can call or even, that I'm not awake yet.... but don't lose any sleep over it. I will call tomorrow, I promise!"

"I believe, I believe," she emphasized the words with a hallelujah persuasion to them.

"And I love your sense of humor McClendon. By the way, what I saw of the exhibit....it's a hell of powerful display and you did a masterful job of putting it together. You're the one who's really, as you said, wonderment personified. Got to go, bye now."

"Jack!... "

"Yes?"

"Be careful!"

"Plan to... over and out," and he was gone.

She sat holding the phone for a few minutes, as if holding the phone would hold on to him. And then it rang and she answered, "Yes," somewhat expectantly.

"When did you start answering with... yes?" It was Greta. "I've been trying to get through all morning. Have you tried to call him yet?"

"Sorry, I suppose I thought it was him calling back. Yes, I did reach him and we just now got off the phone." She looked at the clock. "Yikes, it was almost two hours."

"Geez, your phone bill!"

"No, his phone cards."

"Are you feeling okay about everything?"

"Oh, Greta, everything is super. I'm going to take some time off. Ready for this... I'm going to Singapore this week."

"Are you serious? You're not, you aren't!"

"Yes, I've got to see about taking some of my vacation. I'm going to try to leave Tuesday."

"Oh, come on Gage, that's not possible. Your vacation time isn't a problem, but getting the tickets and packing, it's not just a trip to the Poconos or something... you're talking about halfway around the world."

"I know, I can hardly wait."

"What's this guy got? You're the most level headed human being I know, this is unreal."

"Admittedly," Gage sighed. "But hell, Greta it feels good."

"Well okay then, go for it. Wish I had something half as exciting going on. All I've got is a mid-life crisis husband with the hots for an old girlfriend."

They talked about Mike. Gage tried to convince her that there would be another life out there, if things didn't turn around with him. Greta wasn't buying it. She kept repeating that having two kids didn't exactly put her in the most desirable category for a Mr. Right. For Greta's sake, Gage managed to bridle the enthusiasm that was bubbling inside her own body.

After Greta's phone call, Gage automatically dialed Frank, something she always did when she was leaving town. Then she stopped... it was a such a strong habit having him take care of Pancho... too late, the phone was already ringing.

"Yea," his familiar greeting.

"Hi, I was going to ask you to watch my cat, but since I don't have one anymore, do you have time for a cup of coffee?"

"That's the strangest proposition I've ever had," he laughed. "I'm just putting some finishing touches on a folio, so good timing, I'll be over shortly. Want me to pick up pastries or something?"

"Yeah, bring me the biggest, gooey eclair you can find, in fact bring me two."

His curiosity peaked. Gage ordering over-the-top high cholesterol times two. He thought about it sitting in the bakery drive thru line and thought about it some more while stopped at those dang red lights that always happen when you're in a hurry. He knew it had to have something to do with the dude from Nam. But ordering two eclairs...some people eat sweets when they're stressed and some don't eat at all. So it was either real good or real bad.

She had the coffee made by the time Frank arrived with the white paper sack of flaky pastries. The eclairs were fat and full of vanilla custard and Gage gulped down a first bite even before pouring their coffee. She ate a whole eclair while Frank sat looking at her in disbelief.

"What on earth is going on in your life? You, the quintessential salad girl... stuffing your face with French bakery goods!"

Because the delicacies were so incredibly rich, she reached a satiation point real fast and settled back with a cup of coffee. Then she began to fill Frank in on these last few days since her unfortunate performance at the end of the photography session. She was effervescent and upbeat as she narrated the Jakarta-Chicago telephone epic and she was positively glowing as she spoke of this pilot... the pilot who obviously gave her the glow.

He listened without saying much. He could feel his best friend slipping away from the closeness of their relationship, he knew it was selfish on his part to want to keep things just the way they were. She never made judgements or told him to check his ego at the door. She was always there to listen when he got burned in some of the quirky relationships that he drew like lightening to a lightening rod. Realistically, she deserved to move in a new direction and he needed to put aside self-serving motives and be happy for her. They sat at the kitchen table drinking coffee and enjoying the rain channeling little streams of water down the window.

The relative quiet of their reflectiveness was interrupted by the door bell. Gage rose slowly so as not to break the spell of the water show and went to answer the door.

"Elliott?" she spoke his name in puzzlement.

"Can I come in?" he asked while stepping inside the door.

Before she could answer, he told her that he'd been thinking about her a lot and a rainy Sunday afternoon seemed to be a good time to follow up on it. She stepped back giving him a wide berth while her mind raced to frame a quick reply. She needn't have wasted any thought on it, because instantly from behind came, "Hi, I'm Frank Beccaccio."

It was all she could do to resist the impulse to throw her hand across her forehead in a my hero pose like the silent screen vamp being rescued on the railroad track. But even as Frank spoke, she was sensitive enough to want to spare Elliott total embarrassment.

"Frank, this is Elliott Brandenberg, we worked together a few years ago."

They shook hands somewhat awkwardly.

She reached over and took Frank's hand, "Elliott, Frank is my special friend." She emphasized special and hoped Frank would hang with her on it.

"Sorry," Elliott apologized. "Should have known there was a reason I couldn't get a reading on you, Gage."

"It's okay, Ell. Want a cup of coffee?" She hoped he wouldn't but she felt the need to offer.

He declined and left abruptly. Frank wouldn't let him off the hook quite so easily. "You know don't you, if I hadn't been here, you'd have had a major problem with that dick head."

"You sound like Greta, she can't stand him. I've known him a long time and keep wanting to believe he's a good person... but lately, he's given even me the creeps. Thanks for being a 'bud' and helping me out."

He teased her a little. "Tell your friend, that your old buddy saved you for him. Tell your flyboy over there that he owes me a drink."

Bringing the attention back to her explanation of last weeks events relaxed her and Elliott dropped off the horizon of her thoughts. She finally got around to telling Frank that she was going to try to get a flight to Singapore on Tuesday.

"This coming week?" he was stunned. "I wasn't taking this international fling seriously enough. You're flying to Singapore... this coming week. Hell, you only met this guy a little over a week ago."

"When you say it like that, it doesn't ring right, I know. But it is right... and yes, I'm going to Singapore this week... and yes, I can hardly wait."

Frank poured out the cold coffee and refilled their cups with fresh, expensive smelling dark coffee and raised his cup in a toast, "to the sweetest lay in Singapore."

"You're a bitch, Frank, a regular bitch," she giggled.

"That's what friends are for," he sang out bringing his deep voice up to soprano range. "I'd better get out of here so you can concentrate on matters of the heart... namely international flight connections. By the way, if it doesn't work out... I know this guy in Singapore, nice guy... "

She stopped him. "Go on, get out of here," she gave him a playful shove toward the door. "And if I don't get to talk to you before I go... well, life is good."

He left talking to himself. She heard him say something about a lucky son of a bitch.

20

Tomorrow came. Her mother would have called it a dervish whirlwind. Her mother, bless her soul, called anything that dealt with high energy, a dervish whirlwind. This time Mom would have been close. First she shocked Mr. Espinosa with a short notice request for vacation time, but that went smoothly. Singapore, he couldn't quite understand. Was she sort of being kidnaped, he questioned? She realized just how mundane her life must be, for there to be so much excitement about this little departure from her everyday routine. Word spread through the Gallery taking on a life of its own. Soon she was moving to India and marrying a mercenary. There wasn't enough time to set everyone straight, she would leave that up to Greta. Although, Greta was probably a source of some of the embellishments. Gage left them to enjoy themselves and went to her desk to begin what would become a complicated task of getting a flight at such short notice.

And it really was a problem. She worked hard at getting a ticket on line without any success at all. So she got on the telephone and hung on like a bulldog until she found a sympathetic young man who understood how serious she was in getting to Singapore by Thursday afternoon. She pled her case with all the emotion and distress that she felt he could handle and he stayed with her over an hour searching and back tracking and searching again… and finally, bingo, he found a seat on a flight out of Los Angeles International that would put her in Singapore Thursday afternoon, Singapore time. She had him book a connecting flight from O'Hare to LAX. That part was a breeze, Chicago to Los Angeles flights were about as easy as catching a taxi.

Her co-workers stopped by to wish her a safe trip and several of them patted her on the shoulder and told her how glad they were to see her looking so happy. With tickets confirmed and bon voyages over, she double timed it through a department store clicking off the list she'd put together last evening. Twenty eight dollars and seventy six cents… had to be a record low in getting ready for an transcontinental trip.

On the way home she thought of Mrs. Giovanni, the poor lady would be hurt if she found out second hand that her neighbor had run off to the other side of the world without telling her. She knocked on her neighbor's door. "Hi," she said as Mrs. Giovanni opened the door. "I just wanted to let you know that I'm going on vacation to Singapore tomorrow and ask if it would it be too much trouble to water the plants in my kitchen window? I think you still have my key."

"First the cat goes, and now you," was all she said, without acknowledging the scope of Gage's travel plans.

"Well, there is a difference. I'm not dying!"

"Okay, sure," the words came out slightly slurred and Gage noticed that the little lady was slightly under the influence.

"Where's Mr. Giovanni?" Gage asked politely.

"Watchin' the ball game, where he is all the time, watchin' the friggin' ball game."

"Tell him goodbye for me," she instructed and hurried away before she learned more than she really cared to at this point.

She unlocked the door quickly, listening keenly but heeding Jack's words that she not get uptight waiting for his call. The realization that she was actually leaving tomorrow began to take on critical proportions. Pack lightly…she intended to take only what she could carry on the plane. Airlines changes, baggage claims, and customs lines made that an easy determination. Strangely enough, this junket didn't take much more prep time than a week end trip. In a short time she'd picked out a few easy to pack, easy to wear pieces of clothing, and the much anticipated phone call came through.

"Hello," she said cheerily.

"Hello, to you."

What was it about him, that all he had to do was say hello and suddenly every part of her body became jelly. What was it about him that made her say something stupid like, "you called!"

What she couldn't know was the apprehension that he'd felt in the last twenty four hours. What if something did happen to trans world phone service from this part of the world, not likely, but… the remote possibility kept creeping into his head. So it was with more gladness than she would ever know, that this particular connection was made.

They prattled on, nothing in particular, just happy to be in touch, happy to hear each others voice and very happy indeed, with the flight schedule that Gage had been able to put together on short notice. Jack did remind her again that he had a food supply haul to one of the tiny Indonesian islands, one of the seventeen thousand islands, or some huge number like that.

"Hey, it's okay," now it was her turn to show a confidence level. "I'll be at the airport, and I'll stay at the airport until you show up."

"Cool," was his answer. "By the way Changi, or Singapore International, is one of the best airports in the world. It's one airport where you actually don't mind spending a few hours. It's customer friendly and has exceptional amenities. However, we're not planning on you spending much time there."

"Jack, I'm okay with myself, at this point to say out loud and mean it... that this is the most exciting event of my life."

"Don't limit it to this, luv, the curtain's just going up and it's gonna' be a long run, I promise you. Oh, and before I forget, there are terminals one and two at Changi. You'll be coming in at terminal one and I'll meet you outside customs. There's a glass wall separating those coming through customs from those of us waiting on passengers, so it's a you can see, but just can't touch situation. Never thought much about it until now... now I'm thinking it's not such a good design feature."

"Is there anything, I can bring you?"

"Is that supposed to be a joke?"

She laughed, "well, I meant... batteries, film, etc."

"This is an international marketplace, Ms. McClendon," he chuckled. "Look, I've got to finish up some company paperwork and get it faxed in, so I'm going to have to cut short this call. Unless, you've got any questions, I'll see you in Singapore on Thursday."

"I'm through. It's Singapore on Thursday," she repeated.

There was a certain amount of security in both their minds now and they were able to concentrate on their immediate tasks. Still, she moved her passport a dozen times looking for the best place to remember it tomorrow. Then she turned in early trying to get ahead on sleep, she'd never been a good in-flight sleeper.

Jack finished his paperwork, went to the airport and got tickets on two flights, just in case and then walked over to a canteen, where a group of expatriates hung out playing blackjack. Jenk Wesley was lead mechanic for Global's plane in Jakarta, as a matter a fact, he was their only mechanic. But Jenk hadn't always been a mechanic. He was a carrier pilot, a top gun Navy guy who lost an eye in a hunting accident back in Wisconsin. His life was about flying and about flying only. And once that wild blue yonder addiction got hold of him, nothing much else mattered a whole hell of a lot. He never married, he came close a few times but the idea of competing with a sheet metal mistress didn't set well with his women. One eyed, he was grounded but it didn't discourage him from looking for another niche in the aviation field. If he couldn't fly them, he'd learn the mechanics. Not many pilots could make that kind of transition, but they weren't Jenk Wesley. What better support system could a pilot have than a mechanic who knew both cockpit and maintenance. And, because they tended to fly out of places where requisitioning parts was an oxymoron, Jenk was what you might call a creative mechanic. Jack shuddered to think of makeshift parts that he'd flown on... always successful though. Still it had to be a real bummer for the poor guy, so Jack took him along in second seat as often as possible.

"Hey, Callahan, what's up?" good eye side caught Jack as soon as he walked in.

"Finish your game, and I'll buy you a beer."

"Man, it's time for me to sit out, I'm down five hundred. What's goin?" Jenk eased his big frame down on a stool next to his friend.

"I met someone," Jack eased the words out slowly.

"No, shit? Local?"

"No, Chicago, damn it. Not local enough."

"I'd say you make pretty good use of your time, hoss. This just happen?

"I first met her back in Nam. Remember the gal I showed you in an old copy of the *Stars and Stripes*? The photo where we were all toasting a bunch of short timers."

"Big old city, Chicago, and you just happen to run into a dame you knew thirty years ago. Whee, daddy, you can do better than that. Sounds like my old Maggie story, told my buddies I'd just met her, when she hit me with a palimony suit the next week. And for the life of me, I can't remember why I even told them that to begin with, we'd been screwing around at least ten years. Hell, I thought it was her that didn't want to get married. Back to you, mate... really just ran into her, huh?"

"Okay, I chased her down. Found her in a little town in Missouri, and... well, I'm meeting her in Singapore tomorrow afternoon."

Jenk reared back on his stool, "Jackson, I like your style, Chicago last week, Singapore tomorrow. What about the haul in the morning? We can't cancel, it came in as urgent. Mudslide this one said. I went with you to fly a pallet out there last month and I don't remember enough hills on that island to have a critical mudslide, but that's how the requisition read."

"Want to go again tomorrow?"

"I'd love to good buddy, but I promised Buck I'd work on The Stripper's radio tomorrow morning, get it ready before he gets back from up North."

Buck was in Thailand at a get together of retired overseas government people. His wife died of pancreatic cancer a few years ago while he was part of the embassy staff in Indonesia and he opted to stay in the area after his retirement. Before she got sick, he was building an airplane and he was putting so many hours in on it, that supposedly she told him it would be more believable if he'd told her that he was spending all that time with a stripper or something to that effect. So in due time, the plane was christened, The Stripper. Since then, there have been several other Strippers and Buck Rainbolt had become a regular fixture around the hanger area, giving flying lessons or ferrying corporate people around the area.

"I've got to get some things together so I can leave as soon as I get back tomorrow," Jack commented. " I got seats on a couple of flights, so I can cover my bases if, for some reason it takes longer to unload than normal."

"Makes her sound pretty dang important."

"Yep," was all Jack had to say as he paid for the drinks and left in the direction of the hotel. He stopped at the hotel desk and picked up his laundry. They would bring it up later, but he saw it stacked on a laundry cart and he didn't need anyone bothering him tonight. He fooled around awhile putting a few items in his flight bag and then decided to hit the sack early. He didn't usually have much trouble sleeping… but this evening, one guy in a faraway hotel tossed and turned and thought about tomorrow way too long.

Nature doesn't take lightly to messing with its regimen, so it added a little more sleep to his morning than usual and he had to hurry to keep the flight schedule. Even so, it turned out that he was there before the plane was loaded and had time for a cup of coffee and a little more razzing from Jenk.

"Morning JC, there's been a change in your destination. You're going to Dili this morning," Jenk sounded serious.

He took the paperwork from Jenk while figuring flight time and unloading time in his head, and concluded real fast that this wasn't a day he wanted to fly to West Timor. Jenk let him go on for a few minutes, but even the 'Jenkster Jokester' couldn't bear to ruin his friend's happiness. "Forget it, big guy, just teasing, read before you rant."

"You fool," Jack shrugged it off in good humor. "Last chance, wanna' go with me."

"Nope, not this time. Got your cell phone, buddy? Call me, if you can't get back in time, I'll be happy to stand in for you."

"You didn't screw up my plane, did you?"... Jack's laughter trailed off in the whine of a big airbus taking off. He finished checking the load and got in line for take off. While waiting his turn, he thumbed through the requisition papers. Whoever made the requisition had forgotten to get an authorization signature on it, meaning the company auditors would raise hell over the discrepancy. Too late to worry, it was his turn to go, he pulled the plane up, faced the sun and headed out over the water. This was his drive to work in the morning and he never took the wonder of it for granted. He felt a great deal of humility at being able to live out his passion all his life.

21

The other passengers must have had the same intent to by-pass the baggage carousels, Gage really had to hunt through the overheads to find space for her overnighter. More time was spent cramming than waiting for takeoff. Hers was the middle seat between a window that was wasted on a sleeping airman and an aisle seat bulging with the hulk of a pimply faced young man. Not much wiggle room there, so she mentally downsized and kept as still as possible, passing up the in-flight snacks and taking only a cup of coffee.

She read the back-of-the-seat literature, napped awhile and waited for the pilot's customary... welcome to the city... the temperature is...etc., speech. Time passed surprisingly fast, and Los Angeles suddenly appeared beneath the plane. None too soon, she needed desperately to stretch. Her portly seat buddy didn't interpret the urgency of her discomfort and he sat forming his own gridlock until the entire back of the plane was empty. The airman wasn't inconvenienced because he didn't come alive until the silence of the surroundings awakened him.

Gage enjoyed traveling. In airports, there were curious happenings and it was the ultimate in people watching. She had considerable time between this flight and the international one, so she spent the hours exploring the surrounds, finally having a meal, and then walking to balance the long sit down time ahead. There was an intriguing parade of all shades of people on the planet in and in every conceivable manner of attire. Airport 101 should be a required course study for anthropologists and psychologists.

She lingered on the details of some of the most bizarre travelers. The turbaned Eastern Indian man with a slick Italian suit and toe rings on his sandaled feet... two elderly ladies, obviously twins, identical with their bouffant pink-gray hair, big hoop earrings, and double knit pant suits... the body builder guy with shaved head, eyebrows, and body hair, who was obsessed with his reflection in the plate glass windows, they were that fabric of diversity that never disappointed her.

The boarding call for the Singapore flight spawned a flurry of activity in the passenger area. And again the same routine, finding overhead storage then excusing yourself over and over while trying to work your way to your seat. This time, thankfully, she was in an aisle seat.

A dichotomy of thoughts kept running around her head...you're either mad, as in hydrophobia mad or this is the most wonderful experience in the world. It was eerie to think how hard it was to tell the difference. Think positive, she told herself more than once. Think positive would probably be an operative word on this flight, as there was a woman of a religious order sitting in the seat next to her looking happy and... positive. They introduced themselves before take off, the woman was Sister Esther Concetta, an American, a Catholic nun, who was on her way back to Singapore where she worked in a children's home. Mercifully, she wasn't a motor mouth, and when she did say something it was quite interesting.

Gage began to come down to a real weariness as the plane settled into the familiar drone of massive jet engines working to hold a giant metal cocoon in the air. Around her, a half dozen different movies played out on screens on the backs of seats, through earphones and mostly to passengers already asleep. She reclined the seat, pulled a blanket up over her face, and plummeted into a sleep that lasted nearly half of the transoceanic trip.

He was in the air as well. Only his was a short flight, a mercy flight. Jack had no idea how many of these relief missions he'd flown over the years. It was a given that he loved flying, but deep down he also cared about making a difference. Whether it was medicine, food, or clothing, it took so little to bring a long lost smile to a suffering face. He didn't see the mudslide area as he circled the cracked runway that the French built years ago. There wasn't a large population here, lack of vital resources had pushed them on to more productive areas. It was almost one hundred percent Muslim and most of these islanders were fanatical supporters of the Indonesian President. Many of them belonged to self proclaimed suicide squads who thought they were protected by magic charms and spells. They'd been extremely proactive lately with their leader facing parliamentary censure and Jakarta was preparing for an influx of their radical element in an imminent showdown ahead.

The islanders had been warm and deeply appreciative when he and Jenk flew some critical medical supplies out to them last month. They'd even lined the runway to greet them. This time there was no one in sight, as Jack scanned the ground below. But there was a priority code on the requisition order, so he sat the plane down gently and taxied in toward a rickety building.

He sat for a moment penciling in his log before looking for helpers to unload the food packs, then he hopped down and started toward the building. It would be classic Murphy's law for it to be a holy day here and he couldn't get the plane unloaded. Pushing the screen door open, he stepped inside and called out... no answer, no sound at all inside. But in the same instance, from the area of the plane, there was movement. He turned just in time to see two AK-47 totin' quasi insurgents, one making his way into the plane's cockpit and the other circling the perimeter zeroing in toward the building.

Hell, it was a set-up... a god damned slick set-up. There was no mudslide, a phony requisition... an infiltrator somewhere in the system. He could see movement in the cockpit. "You sons of a bitches," he mumbled as he crawled through an unscreened window and ran for the scrubby foliage at the back of the building. He glanced back while trying to work his way up to a rocky knoll. They hadn't fired the AK-47's and there had to be a reason. He didn't much like the reason that kept surfacing in his mind. It had to be that a damn suicide squad needed food somewhere and they needed him to get it to them. Makes sense now, no signature on the request papers. He quit thinking and started moving, he could see the hunter nearing the knoll. It had been a long time since survival school and they didn't teach use of a cell phone in a crisis situation, but he knew his only chance other than cooperating with those fanatics was to get in touch with Jenk.

He moved as fast as he could to put some distance between them so he could try the phone. He was in dense foliage fraught with vines now and any speed at all sent him reeling when he snagged on one. As if that wasn't enough, the giant leaves smacked him hard to add a further insult. Whether the cell phone would even work... couldn't think that way, it had to work, he steeled himself. He couldn't see his adversary at this point, so he melted into a big cluster of ornery vines and dialed the numbers of what had to be the most urgent phone call of his life. He literally did not breathe until finally he heard, "Jenk here."

Jenkin Wesley didn't like to be interrupted in the middle of his repair procedures. He was holding two radio wires in his hand when the phone rang and he took his time marking them before he answered with the nonchalance that was his trademark.

"Jenk, listen up," Jack's voice sounded serious. "The flight was a set-up. I've got at least two friends here with AK-47's. One's in the plane, and the other's playing tag with me. I'm not dead, so they must need me to fly a hijacked food load."

"Shit, man, what's the plan?"

"Can you, uh... bring The Stripper? You can put it down at the edge of the water where there's a rusty hull sticking out. Remember? I'll be in the brush area somewhere near the hull and I'll be watching. If you don't see me by the time you set down, get the hell out of here! See you later buddy. Gotta go, chase man's coming."

Jenk yelled back, "You carrying anything?"

"I've got a Glock." With that he snapped the phone back onto his belt and reached down to free the Austrian made Glock from his ankle strap. He'd never fired the pistol in a civilian capacity, but then he'd never come face to face with the business end of an AK-47. He could see the glint of steel in the neighborhood now, so he decided to lead the gunman away from Jenk's landing site. He'd have to move the guy pretty quickly North and then double time it back in order to catch his ride. Trying to find your way and watch your tail at the same time was no easy task, but Jack didn't intend to lose either physically or mentally. He kept his plan in sharp focus as well as keeping a keen eye on his stalker and silently they moved in tandem through the undergrowth.

While Jack was moving his man up north, Jenk was processing what he'd just heard on the phone. He'd just heard his friend calling on him for help... him, a one eyed son of a gun who hadn't flown a plane in fifteen years and didn't have a license anymore... and the only available plane had a inoperable radio and belonged to someone out of the country. He mulled it over for a minute, felt that old rush of excitement and the game was on. He threw his toolbag out the door, checked the gas and taxied The Stripper out of the hanger. Buck Rainbolt's plane was a pampered lady, but this was going to be a hussy trip. CGK was a busy major airport and he couldn't communicate with the tower, so he taxied as far away from the traffic as he could get, turned his good eye both directions, caught a clear spot and simply lifted off in between the big guys. He couldn't help but smile, every pilot wants to pull a stunt like that, but its not worth losing a license over. Guess what, he thought to himself... can't lose what you don't have. He cleared the pattern and headed toward his buddy. "Give me twenty minutes, big guy," he said aloud. In his mind, he went over JC's words to see if he could glean anything else from them. But the conversation was so short, he was sure he had it all... two guys, AK-47's, pick up point at boat hull. The last sentence... get the hell out if he was a no show, wouldn't wash with Jenk. Couldn't leave a good guy stranded, no way, no how. He pushed Buck's sweet flying lady real hard and she responded nicely.

Jack was getting concerned about the timing. He needed to head back so he tried a quick lateral move to get far enough to the side to permit some backtracking. Suddenly, out of nowhere, he had an AK-47 between his shoulder blades. The damn bastard had second guessed him. He couldn't see him, but he could tell from the voice that this bush fighter was young and pumped full of adrenaline, a highly volatile combination. Jack walked passively, not creating any kind of scene whatsoever and taking periodic jabs to the kidney area in silence. He knew better than to incite the fanatic further so he tuned out the unintelligible rhetoric and concentrated on a way out. He ducked a vine which snapped back into the gunman's face and thought for a moment that it was going to cost him his life. The cost turned out to be a little less, a swift hard blow to his left shoulder, but it convinced him that whatever action he decided to take, it had better work...there wouldn't be a second chance.

Time was getting critical now. Jenk was going to drop down out of the sky pretty soon and not have a passenger waiting, if he didn't do something shortly. They came to a rocky downhill pass and the young radical was shoving the gun hard at him, Jack could feel him actually leaning into his back. He picked up the pace some, then as the incline got steeper, Jack foiled his follower with a swift jump to the right and a left leg flung sideways to make a beautiful hurdle.

The AK-47 went over first followed by a human tumbling block. The gunman lost his weapon trying to keep his head from bouncing off a jagged rock. Before he could regain his balance, Jack snatched up the AK and changed places with his captor who quickly recognized the plight of the situation and stayed squatting on the ground. It was hard to tell who was sweating more, they were both drenched. For the first time, Jack spoke to his adversary, "Where's your protection, where's your magic spell, huh? Up," he demanded, waving the spoils of his victory, the AK-47. As the steely faced insurgent got to his feet, Jack motioned for him to remove his belt. "Ah, a perfect belt for tying, thanks partner," he taunted. "You made a couple of mistakes, bonehead. The first was following me entirely too closely and the second.... you, bastard, you didn't take my gun. Did you hear me? You didn't even take my gun." He knew the backwoods soldier didn't understand a word he was saying, but it didn't matter. He laid the 47 on the ground and with the Glock in his captive's backside he walked him to a small tree, backed him up against it and belted him just above his elbows tightly to the tree.

"Have a nice day!" he shouted as he picked up the AK-47 and made tracks for the edge of the island as fast as he could. He could feel his heart pounding hard in the aftermath of the encounter. "What the hell am I doing at my age?" ran over and over in his mind like a mantra as he darted around vines and through the undergrowth. If he figured right, and if Jenk didn't have complications, he should hear The Stripper coming in soon. He mobilized all the energy he could muster, didn't want to miss the pick up. It wasn't long before he could see clearing. He came out of the tree covering on a small bluff where he could see the boat hull. It was still a good half mile away. He turned back into the brush and started a breakneck dash toward the old boat skeleton.

Out of nowhere and in absolute silence, The Sripper glided in low and headed for the pick up point. What a friend! As soon as Jack spotted the plane with the engine off, it gave him a real lift and a second wind as he sprinted along the savannah at the edge of the thicket. Such a buddy, a bonafide good samaritan, he didn't want Jenk in danger, so he maxed those last few yards.

The plane was on the ground for a couple of minutes before Jack popped out of the tree line and ran toward it carrying a shiny souvenir. "Damn it to hell, you know how to make a man pee in his pants," was Jenk's reaction at the shock of an AK-47 coming at him out of the bushes. He moved over, "Good to see you in one piece, you can take her home!"

Jack started the engine and they were rolling fast along the hard packed sand when the familiar clack, clack, clack of small arms fire strafed across the horizon. They heard the heart sinking sound of metal ripping... racking the plane... wounding Buck's pretty lady .

"Shit, man... the rudder... the god damned rudder," Jenk yelled as a cross wind hit them making it a struggle to keep the plane away from the boat hull coming up fast in front of them. If Jack could pull up hard enough they were okay, otherwise it was sayonara. Neither breathed....both were intensely locked in a mental willing of crucial lift for the plane. A cross wind was not exactly the best complement to rudder problems. They were right on top of the hull, Jenk said later that you couldn't pull dental floss between them.

Beads of perspiration trickled down Jack's forehead, it literally was a manual effort that he managed to pull the plane over that old boat frame. Jenk reached over and wiped his friend's brow as the adept dragon man vied to get the plane aloft and level. The gunner was still firing at their backside, but they were beyond his reach now. "Guess he wasn't gettin' any target practice guarding the food," Jack said. He looked over at Jenk and saw a very pale individual.

Jenk saw the glance. "You know, don't you buddy, I couldn't have done it. One eye in a close game like this is a incapacitating disability. As Jenk talked, his color came back, then his sense of humor. "Okay Air Force, you win the flying game, but man, you lose big time on personal hygiene. You look like hell and you smell like crap."

Callahan looked down. His pants and shirt were soaked with perspiration. The dirt had turned to mud and in the closeness of the cockpit, there was a definite locker room stench. He apologized, that was about all he could do. The Stripper headed home smooth and easy. He'd flown more than one mission in Nam with rudder problems, rather have it shot up than jammed.

"What happened back there?" Jenk prodded.

"It was the damndest thing. First of all it looks like we were snookered by a phony requisition order. You know, I didn't see any civilians on the island. The bastards must have had them contained somewhere. And I only saw two guerrillas, they could have mowed me down and didn't, so I suspect that I was probably going to be their delivery boy ."

"What about the owner of that AK-47?" Jenk nodded toward the gun.

"He's picnicking real close to a little tree."

"Not by choice, I take it."

"Right, not by choice," Jack relaxed a little. "I didn't hurt him. He had the AK in my back and he was leaning on me working our way down a rocky path. The chance came up and I tripped him, tied him with his belt to a tree and brought you a trophy."

"Well, Jackson, sir, I'm duly impressed," Jenk saluted jauntily.

"Thanks, impressing you wasn't on my mind, getting to Singapore was though."

"You just may not make it, we're ten minutes out... and pal, you've already missed the first plane you were booked on, and the second flight leaves the gate in about thirty minutes."

Jack was silent, he was going to Singapore one way or another. They entered the traffic pattern and waited their turn. Without a radio, he couldn't communicate with the tower, but it didn't look like directional stability was going to be a landing problem, winds were okay. " Will you take The Stripper over to the hangar and do what you can to get the plane fixed. I'll be back in a few days and I'll settle up with you then." He felt for his wallet. It was still there, his passport was always in his wallet. Then he turned his head to the rear seat real quick. "Hey bud, how about handing me that carton of cigarettes?" He pointed to the unopened Marlboroughs laying half hidden under a newspaper.

JC wasn't and never had been a smoker so Jenk came back with, "Okay who're you bribing?"

"I'm going to try to buy me a ride up to the gate."

"Are you crazy, you're going to Singapore like that?" he held his nose mockingly. "What about your flight bag, it's in the hangar?"

"The airport has clothing shops and work-out centers with showers, not a problem."

"Alright how about this problem. They might not let you on the plane. They just might think you're some kind of stinky subversive. As a matter of fact, we both could be persona non grata here at the airport. I took off without clearance," Jenk said casually as they began a stiff descent.

"Could be," Jack responded looking around. "But I don't see any militia with guns pointed at us. How am I on time now?"

"Well, I suspect they're just about ready to board, and may have already started."

Landing was sluggish but thankfully uneventful. Jack taxied straight over to a follow-me truck where a worker was parked and taking a food break. He grabbed the cigarettes from Jenk, shook hands, and hopped out, "Thanks a bunch pardner'. I'll call the office tomorrow."

"Give her one for me," Jenk's words rang out behind him.

"Screw you," he laughed as he walked toward the truck . The Indonesian driver looked like a caricature in slow motion. His brow was furrowed with bewilderment while his food filled mouth hung low and open. The grungy pilot approached the truck, showed his tickets to the worker and indicated as best he could the urgency of time. There wasn't much reaction until Jack indicated payment with the carton of cigarettes. Suddenly, he had a taker. The driver motioned for Jack to get in the truck and he immediately took on the role of determined courier. Cigarettes were international currency. They moved quickly around the various concourses. To be this close and miss the flight would be hard to take, Jack could see the plane . It was still at the gate, so there was a chance. The expediter had really gotten into their little caper, highly illegal though it probably was, and delivered him to a service door where he tossed the Marlboroughs to the smiling Indonesian and ran into a common area. Just inside the door a Singapore Airlines captain was describing some kind of problem to a hydraulics man when Jack butted into the conversation. "Excuse me," he stretched out his hand showing an identification card, "JC Callahan, pilot with Global Relief." He added, " I'm back late from a mission and am about to miss my flight." He pointed to the big Airbus 310 which was ready to go. Thank goodness for the close camaraderie among pilots. The captain grabbed a phone, called for a hold on the plane and personally escorted him to the gate. Jack threw everything out on the counter.... passport, visa, keys, and tickets while they repositioned the walkway.

"You have baggage?" the employee asked. He thought what she probably wanted to say was, "I hope to god you have other clothes." He turned and shook hands with the Captain.

They got him on board. At least, he was in business class, where the seats were further apart. On the other hand, those who paid the most for their fares, had to share space with what looked to be a first class eccentric, a role further exacerbated by causing the flight delay. As soon as they were at altitude, he went to the lavatory to wash up. Afterwards he sank back in the spacious accommodations and paid no further attention as to whether or not he was a continuing source of curiosity. A professional looking lady in the seat directly across the aisle did ask if he was an anthropologist. Dirt and anthropology, it made sense. He felt obliged to give her a quick synopsis relative to his appearance. She listened intently. But he got the feeling she didn't believe anything he was telling her. So much for that, he stopped talking and tried thinking of the things he'd left in his flight bag. Suddenly, he pulled out his key chain. He'd put the ring he'd bought in Chicago on it for safekeeping. It was there, everything was on track and in a matter of minutes, he was snoozing. He didn't tell the professional looking lady that the sales tag was still hanging under the sleeve of her suit jacket.

22

On the 747 from Los Angeles to Singapore, Gage managed a restful sleep and in the last few hours of the flight had a pleasant conversation with Sister Esther Concetta, the director of a Catholic Children's Center in Singapore. She was intrigued that two strangers brought together in a rather captive situation for a short time felt comfortable enough to confide some rather personal issues to each other. Gage told the sister the entire story of the last two weeks of her life...how an old acquaintance found her, thanks to an art flyer... how they spent the weekend in Ste. Genevieve and even about the horrible muck up at the Gallery that led to this trip to Singapore.

Sister Esther Concetta had an interesting slant on the Gallery disaster. With a musical pitch to her voice, she intoned softly, "Oh, no my dear, it was not a muck up. It allowed both of you to experience extreme despair in your loss of each other. Had you never have reached that level, you might never have known how much you mean to each other."

"Interesting philosophy. I like it. Do you mind if I ask... were you ever in a relationship?"

She addressed the question with slow deliberation, "Yes... yes, a long time ago, but my parents wouldn't accept the young man in my life, as he was a Protestant. They firmly directed me on a path toward the convent."

"Were you broken hearted?"

"Oh yes, I surely thought I'd die. But time passed, my broken heart healed, and you know, this is where I really want to be. I love my work and I love those children. Perhaps, you and your friend might like to drop by and see our Children's Center. The little ones do some terrific art work, I think you would find it a moving experience." Sister Esther Concetta pulled out her business card and delicately handed it to Gage.

"I think it would be great to see your children, what a wonderful idea. I don't know, of course, just what kind of schedule we'll have, but I do promise to try."

The nun put her hand in front of her mouth and with a twinkle in her eye whispered, "Don't go out of your way, if you're busy."

"Well, Sister Esther Concetta," she said in a overdone southern belle dialect, "I do declare, I don't know what you're talking about."

Amidst their laughter, the beverage cart arrived and Gage turned to her new acquaintance with an impromptu, "Would you like a drink?"

"Why yes, thank you. I'd like a bourbon and water."

"Make it two," Gage added. Bourbon wasn't her drink but somehow it seemed felicitous to order the same drinks for both of them. The flight would be coming to an end soon and the good sister and the gallery director thanked each other for making the trip a pleasant experience. In their repartee, Gage suggested that maybe this was a protected flight because of the sister's holy presence.

The response to that particular statement was wholly unexpected as Sister Esther Concetta leaned toward her and in earnest solemnity replied, "You don't actually think I believe all that, do you?" Neither knew where to go next with that conversation, so they simply smiled as if sharing a schoolgirl secret.

Meanwhile the guy who'd been the topic of most of their transoceanic conversation landed at Singapore International. After checking the ETA of the Los Angeles flight, he went directly to one of the upscale clothiers in the terminal. Shopping was easier for him here than in Atlanta because he'd already spent some time looking at mens clothes while on earlier layovers. He started from zero... skivies to shoes. The clerks in the apparel shop were the only people he'd come in contact with since he left Jakarta who didn't do a double take at the state of his clothing. He wasn't sure if it was because they'd seen it all... working in this crossroads of the world or because he was piling the counter full of purchases. He added a piece of soft luggage to the pile, paid up and headed to the fitness center.

It was one of those spa and fitness spots where everyone wore designer work-out clothes and drank designer water. Jack inquired about a presser and a diminutive lady appeared almost instantly. She took his shopping bag, cut the tags off, pressed everything including socks while he showered. Razors were complimentary....the showers were oversized and lavish. An attendant was waiting with an armload of thick towels.

As he pulled a big towel across his back, he could see a substantial bruise in the kidney area. He turned around further in the mirror and didn't find a whole lot of evidence of his morning encounter. A few scrapes and scratches here and there, but generally he'd been pretty darn lucky. The old clothes were discarded and the new clothes, including shoes, felt good.... really good. He packed the extras in the new soft leather bag and headed for the Customs/Immigration area.

He experienced an unusually strong feeling of well being, like he'd paid his dues and now he was eligible to step into the most exciting part of his life. It was almost euphoric and even he was amused at himself.

Jack found the Immigration area intriguing. There was an expansive glass wall separating those coming into the country from those patiently waiting for friends or relatives. You could see, but couldn't touch which made the spontaneity of greetings and the ensuing anticipation dissipate to some degree by the time the passengers were allowed to pass through the transparent barrier. It was unfortunate that even the tiniest bit of that initial enthusiasm was lost. Funny that it never seemed important before. There was an English tabloid newspaper laying on a bench which caught his eye and gave him a chuckle. DO YOU KNOW THAT YOUR LIFE IS ABOUT TO CHANGE were the exact headlines. "Yes I do," he verified his awareness out loud. He didn't have any answers or a plan. He just knew that he had finally found someone so special that he wanted to be a part of her life. It ran through his mind several times, that he was getting soft. It was always, flying first and everything else worked around that….but lately there had been an override of priorities, namely one Gage McClendon and this was the first time in thirty years that he could ever truthfully say that.

One thing about a glass wall and Customs, when they spot checked anyone's luggage it was in full view of an audience. An hour of suitcases being conveyed along the inspection counters kept your attention. Underwear seemed to be the hiding place of choice, apparently so, because more lace panties and boxers shorts were unrolled and given a good shake than any other item coming into the country. There was, however, one item of clothing that caught his attention as the customs people held it in the air. It was red, either a dress or a slip, he couldn't tell which, but the sight of it stirred some powerful remembrances. He could still see the red dress with the thin straps… the dress that clung nicely to her body in the sultry summer night. He could even smell the powerful elixir of perfume and perspiration, seductive and primal… and so deeply etched in his mind. Girl, you have no idea, this is crazy, wonderfully crazy, he mused as he walked over to a cold drink machine. It was a good feeling to think that he still had the need to cool down some. What a day! This morning a machine gun was stabbing into his backside and five hours later flashbacks, not the bad kind… the deliciously erotic flashbacks of two bodies moving into each other, swelling into each other and pulling from that jungle of primitive instincts until the passions were exhaustively soothed.

Realizing his drift of thoughts didn't have much airport relevancy, Jack opted to read a Market Guide that someone left in a nearby chair. Sing Tel Communications, solid company, good price to earnings ratio, he needed to look into it.

LA to Singapore was in the traffic pattern... Gage was as hyper as the four year old sitting two seats ahead. She fidgeted and fumbled with her purse and her new champion of encouragement, Sister Esther Concetta, admonished her to settle down. "Love is patient," she said. But then she added, "I would like to see this man. I think in the vernacular of the youngsters, he must be 'hot'. It's not a term, I'd use myself, but it's one that the young people use a lot lately."

"You won't be disappointed," Gage assured her. "He's the only guy in the world who could drag me across the ocean with no more forethought than I've had." Suddenly, she got clammy. "What if I should have taken more time?"

"Nonsense, you're in love, don't second guess it."

"Is that why my head's spinning, my mouth's dry, and my heart's in overdrive."

"Yea, ain't love grand?" teased the nun. "There's your destination," she added pointing through the window as the wheels touched the pavement and the big plane began braking down the runway. They rolled up to the concourse and immediately began to disembark.

Gage gave the nun a big hug, "Have you got something you can say for me on that rosary?"

"You relax, I'll take care of it for you," the sister assured her.

As she walked into the International Immigration and Customs area Gage heard a voice behind her call out, "Ms. McClendon."

She turned to see Sister Esther Concetta with her hands cupped to her mouth and calling out, "You, go girl!"

What a cool nun! She hadn't been around women of religious orders very much and certainly didn't expect the sense of humor that she'd found in this gal. The sight of the woman in perfectly sensible clothes and perfectly sensible shoes calling out, "You go, girl," was so out of character that Gage had to smile and as a result she began to relax. In retrospect, the clever sister was smart enough to have purposely orchestrated the little scenario just to break the tension for her.

The daydreaming ended... reality was on the other side of the glass and he saluted her in a relaxed, unhurried way. She saw what he meant when he'd described the glass wall. What a bummer, she'd rather not see him until she could see him close up and personal. Thankfully, they weren't doing many luggage checks. They took a second look at her passport, no idea why, but they eventually handed it back to her. One of the few spot checks done was on the man's luggage just in front of her. You always think there must be something that throws up a red flag, but who knows. In this case, the man's things were squeaky clean.

She grabbed her bag as soon as she was cleared, took a deep breath and walked into the arms of Major JC Callahan. Her first words, "Have you been waiting long?"

His words, "Yes… thirty years." He reached out and took her hand and brought her close to him where they stood entranced, looking deep into each others eyes… past now… past Singapore. And they must have liked what they saw, they smiled. Jack moved his fingers across her face as if reading her in braille and her face gave back something radiant and intoxicating. He slipped the Chicago gift on the ring finger of her left hand while their hearts beat to an intense rhythm coming from deep in the soul. And then he broke the spell….he picked her up and twirled her around. It was then, that they laughed. It was then that the ring caught a glint of light and showed off a dazzling sparkle and it was then that they laughed some more.

It was also, then…that a laughing Sister Esther Concetta caught the eye of her new friend and gave her a thumbs up before disappearing into the crush of travelers to tend the world's children. And the radiant couple who was going for the next life cycle strolled hand in hand through Singapore International Airport.

Ravel's Bolero was playing on the airport music system. Gage glanced at the handsome man beside her. Nah… he didn't… he couldn't have… .

And Jack Callahan… he just smiled.

23

The next few days were much like a fantasy world. Each morning flowed smoothly into evening. The historic Raffles Hotel near the center of the city was the base for daytime excursions, theaters, and late dinners. It was also a mecca that drew them back time and time again... where solidly cloistered, they could revisit the enthusiasm of their new relationship.

"Come on lets go down to the Padang and pay homage to the Thomas Raffles statute," Jack called out to Gage early one morning.

"Same name as the hotel?"

"A friend of Singapore's. A really good friend, apparently. There are parks, statutes, and schools named after him. I think he came here in the 1800's to set up a trading post for the British East India Company when there was nothing here but swamps and malaria. Great foresight. So the center of the city is called Raffles Place. Come on," he said taking the empty cup from her hand, "let's go say hello to old Tom and do some rubbernecking. And hey, the Singapore Art Museum is full of outstanding Asian modern art."

The mention of an art museum quickened her pace as they walked along the gracious corridors. Jack gave a little history of the hotel as they made their way toward the main lobby. "This place has a tremendous provenance. Over the years famous residents such as Kipling, Somerset Maugham and Joseph Conrad idled away their time here. And in 1904, a circus tiger was killed as it crouched under a billiard table."

She listened intently as he went on with the history. "The Singapore Sling was supposedly first concocted here. Now it's an overpriced white elephant of a drink, but everyone wants to try one just to touch on the flamboyant history of the twenties and thirties."

Gage laughed, "Well, why should I be any different. I'll have to try one." Her eyes followed along the shopping arcade as they left the hotel. Make a mental note, she told herself. It looked like a place for some serious shopping... or at least, some serious looking.

They did a lot of walking and also spent considerable time on the city buses and MRT. Singapore had great public transportation. They took the bus to Emerald Hill and saw the prewar homes and shops that were restored in the 1980's. They went to the zoo and to Jurong Bird Park and the incredible modern art museum. They hung out at the

Saxophone, a wonderful outdoor cafe that permeated the evening air with jazz, blues, and light rock. They spent one night in the ambience of Studebaker's glitzy nightclub and even took in the Geylang, the infamous red light district in this city of three million people. They ate lobster curry and tried rendan santan, a coconut flavored chicken dish, and gorged time and time again on wonderful Chinese dishes. It was a surreal time. If ever one believed in a mantel of inspired harmony, the two were surely the resonators of perfection.

One day was spent simply on a mission… that of replacing the red dress…the Ste. Genevieve red dress followed of course by the re-creation of that scenario….starting out somewhat in spoof, but ending on the same level of ecstasy afforded the little Missouri hotel. Only this time, the red dress was spared the fate of endless overhead circles. And while the two depleted bodies became victims of contented meltdown, the dress stayed bright and pure. "Sweetheart, you've been my dream for a long time. And now real life exceeds the dream world. I love you very much," Jack murmured as they lay together…. exhausted but still touching and still wanting to touch.

Gage responded lightly at first with, "Thank you." Then she quickly added, "And I love you… I love you… I love you!!!! I want to take you home with me." However, it was never far from her mind that this wasn't a normal day to day relationship. Jack had a life on this side of the world and she existed quite nicely in a totally different environment.

The days began with sumptuous breakfasts where the dialogues rambled from corny conversations to heavy duty philosophy. "What drives you, Jack? What keeps you in a state of heightened awareness?" Gage pointed a pancake filled fork at him as she talked. "When we're walking on the street, I sense that behind the sunglasses your eyeballs are doing constant surveillance. Yet, to look at you… you have the calmest surface demeanor of anyone I've ever met. Tell me what makes you tick?"

For a brief second that cool demeanor across from her seemed stunned at the perception, then he quickly smiled and answered playfully, "I guess its that old Wyoming 'play it close to your chest' trait that is based on suspicion of everyone and everything. And at this moment, I'm suspicious that you might like to go see your friend's school."

"That's wimping out of a question, but I guess that's all I'm going to get out of you for now... let's go. I'd like to see Sister Esther's children."

"Did you get an address?"

"Yea, she gave me her card."

Jack studied the card. "Interesting. Let's take a taxi. Looks like the school is in Chinatown, further than we'll want to walk. Finish your pancakes... we've got plenty of time."

They were ready for a day out. Gage had her bottled water and a stash of dark chocolates. He had his sunglasses and his ever present cell phone. The phone rang a lot and he joked that he was really placing bets on horses. She assumed it was company business as the conversations always seemed serious, lengthy, and very private.

"Taxi," he called toward the row of vehicles lined up outside the hotel. The first taxi in the line pulled up even with them and Jack opened the car door. He closed it as quickly as he opened it and without saying a word guided Gage to a taxi further back in the line of cabbies.

"Will you please tell me what that was all about?" Gage pleaded.

"Didn't like his looks."

"The driver, are you serious? Didn't like his looks?" she parroted his remarks. "I can't fault your reasoning, you've obviously taken care of yourself a long time and seem to have done a good job of it, but hell, Callahan, you've got more sides than a Rubik's cube."

"Tell me that....that's what you love about me, that I can keep you puzzled. It better be that, cause there's not much else," he bantered jocularly as they slid into the handpicked taxi.

In the midst of their repartee, they realized that the driver was waiting for a destination. "The Sultan Mosque," Jack uttered. The driver looked at them with a look of dismay as he pulled into the traffic. They wove in and out of the lanes and in a very short time were abruptly deposited at the Sultan Mosque very close to their hotel. Gage could see that the driver was as much disappointed with such a short fare as she was confused by their actions. Hand in hand they scampered through the pedestrians and around a corner where Jack flagged down another taxi and handed the driver the Sister's business card. "Okay Ma'am, sit back and enjoy your trip to Chinatown," the winsome pilot encouraged as they situated themselves for the ride to the Sister's school.

"Is there anything I need to know about... something?"

"No, it's s.o.p.," he replied offhandedly.

"Say again?"

"Just short for standard operating procedure. Hey, look. We're coming to the most colorful part of Singapore. The city is essentially Chinese, but Chinatown is more intensely Chinese than the rest of it." He couldn't have been more right. Ahead of them was the full pageantry of a Chinese funeral and they sat mesmerized at the ancient ceremonial pomp and the mystical smell of incense.

The driver followed behind the throng of celebrants giving his sightseers a running commentary along the way. "Sago Lane," he called out as he pointed to a short street on their right. "Chinese Death House, where people go to die, when their time is near."

"It's getting a little too morbid, hope we're near the school," Jack said loudly.

"Pretty soon, sir, pretty soon now," the cabbie announced.

And it wasn't long until they pulled up to the front of the low concrete building, the Catholic Children's Center. They signaled the driver to wait until they could make sure Sister Esther was there. They rang a buzzer and waited several minutes. A diminutive and ancient looking woman opened the door part way. She said nothing. Gage inquired as to whether Sister Esther Concetta was there? The old lady remained silent and gave no indication that she understood. The door closed and they were left to wait… not knowing whether there was any action on the other end of a supposed mission to find the nun. Suddenly the door burst open like a cattle chute.

"My friends, the lovers, come on in," a cheery voice called out. "I'm so glad you came, oh my goodness. Kwan, put the tea on and bring some orchids from the back garden, please." The wordless woman came to life and hustled off to attend to her tasks. The beaming nun squeezed and hugged the visitors as Gage tried to find out whether it was a good day to visit the children. "Of course, it's always a good day to visit the children…and wait until I tell them that a real art director is here. They love art, and by the way they love to dance for visitors. And you my dear," she turned toward Jack, "you're the reason this young lady flew to Singapore? Well," she said stepping back and taking a long look at him, "I think she has good taste, I can tell you're a very kind man, also a very handsome man."

Jack thanked the Sister as he waved the taxi driver off and delighted her with his observation… that she was so complimentary that she must be running for a political office. She liked that. She grabbed him by the arm and they talked briefly about Singapore politics. Before long Kwan showed up with a handsome array of orchids for Gage. Orchids were ordinary garden flowers in Singapore, but Sister Esther knew that the American would find them a very special presentation. The tea arrived covered with a battenberg tea cozy and Kwan set out cups and saucers for a very tidy little party. It was relaxing. They laughed and chatted like old friends.

The children came in with their attendants and bowing low to the visitors began the simple little dances native to Chinese children. Gage was touched by the seriousness of the little dancers. She supposed that each one performed to the best of his or her ability to catch the eye of possible adoptive parents. It was beautiful, but it was also a bit sad. All those children... all those hopeful children. She tried not to choke up. The nun saw her discomfort and decided that they should move on into the art classes.

They spent the entire day at the school. Jack was an active participant in the art classes....and Gage was pleasantly surprised at his expertise. The school was rich in charcoal sticks, so he did a lot of charcoal sketches of the kids. They crowded around him watching, then trying to imitate every flourish and stroke as his fingers moved deftly along the drawing paper.

The good Sister hovered everywhere... praising the children and giving them generous hugs. The afternoon dissolved rapidly into evening when Sister Esther unexpectedly announced that Kwan had prepared dinner for the two guests and they should begin to wind down the art clinic. It brought groans from the kids, they were really enjoying the input from the two Americans.

The guests protested the extra effort of cooking for them. "Sister, we didn't expect to interfere quite so much with your schedule."

"Nonsense, besides Kwan loves to show off her cooking skills. She used to work in a hotel kitchen and she's always trying out some strange named dish on me." About that time Kwan motioned for them to follow her. She led them into the nun's private living area. The table was literally covered with food. Up to this point they had resisted the traditional seven to twelve course meals based on the premise that one stomach shouldn't have to play host to such quantum bulk. It was surrender time now, and they graciously caved into a banquet mode. Sister was right, Kwan was an excellent cook. Malayan food, she explained, is based on various mixtures of spices. Sometimes very unorthodox mixtures... star anise, cardamon, tumeric, and cumin plus all the more common spices... and all in the same dish giving most of the dishes a curried taste.

The nun rummaged around the fridge looking for some Dutch beer that she remembered a priest leaving with her from a visit early in the Spring. "Eureka, I've found drink," she exclaimed, closing the big door of the commercial refrigerator. There were two bottles. Jack was given his own bottle and the gals each had a glass. They teased the nun about a having a priest in her house, and she didn't discourage their playfulness or make excuses for the priest's visit. Gage begged off of the last couple of courses of food, stopping with the deliciously prepared moolie. Jack made his way though all twelve courses...distracted repeatedly by thought of the monstrous work-out that he'd have ahead of him in the hotel tomorrow.

It was late. The stomachs had taken over their brains and conversation was fading fast when Jack's phone rang. His posture suddenly became erect... his mind alert and his thought processes back on track. Gage sensed extreme urgency in his voice. He walked the floor grimacing and running his hand through his hair saying very little. The conversation was terse. He slowly closed the sleek silver cell phone and didn't say anything for a few seconds. He opened the phone again and while dialing said quietly to Gage, "The twin towers of the World Trade Center are gone."

"What do you mean... gone?"

He didn't answer her, but spoke to someone on the other end of his phone. "Hey pardner, about the fishing trip that I was supposed to work. I can't make it. It's a transocean trip, will you take it for me? I've got to tend the roses in my garden the next couple of days." A pause, then, "Thanks, bud. There's a trophy wrapped in brown paper in my room. Open it and make sure that it's the right one." Another pause. "Your contact for the expedition will be at the center for little fisheaters here in Singapore. Stay with this trip as long as it takes." A long sigh followed. "Good fishing, man." The whole conversation took less than a minute.

Gage tried to fathom what she'd just heard. She took his hand which still held the cell phone and shook it gently to break his concentration. He didn't respond immediately. When he did, it was swift. "My friend, Jenk Wesley, is coming to take you back to Chicago. He'll stay with you. And I mean... with you... at your home... or wherever... as long as he thinks there's a need. He has one good eye... he's from Wisconsin... and a gal once sued him for palimony.

Her name was Maggie. Ask him where he's from and the gal's name. If he's one eyed and can answer your questions...do whatever he says. Esther Concetta, can you handle one more guest tonight?"

The Sister nodded affirmatively.

Turning to his dazed friend, he grabbed her and pulled her close saying nothing for a short time, just holding her in his arms. "I'm so... so... sorry. God, I love you so much. I'll see you on the other side"... rethinking his words, he added, "of the pond, that is." With that he shook hands with Sister Esther and disappeared into the night shadows.

24

They stood together facing an empty doorway. It was as if he'd vaporized. He had no transportation at this point...and where he was headed? And why? The Sister turned on a small television in her study to see if they could get some idea of what he'd meant in those quiet words, 'the twin towers of the World Trade Center are gone."

They were paralyzed with the cataclysmic, horrendous nightmare playing out in front of the whole world. The World Trade Center buildings were tragically imploded... taken down by terrorists... thousands of lives crushed beneath tons of concrete and steel. Not in the United States of America... not those imposing twin towers.

Throughout the night they watched CNN International... dozing and waking and disbelieving... .struggling with an ocean of murky emotions. Not the least of which was... what was the vagary connection of the guy who'd just walked out their door, to what the news media was calling an international terrorist attack. Gage felt helpless, "I know he's a good guy, and I don't know why I need to keep repeating that over and over."

"I'm sure he's a good guy," Sister Esther reassured her. Halfway across the building, Kwan sensed something bothersome in the Sister's living quarters. In checking on them she joined the hypnotic vigil. Gage fretted at getting the specifics of Jack's instructions right. And like the movie of repetition, *Ground Hog Day*, the networks replayed the highjacked airliners slamming into the buildings time and time again. And time and time again, they watched in horror.

There was one guy who had no time to become infused with the coverage of the attack. Jenk Wesley had a mission. He was in the hotel having a beer with a member of the British Consulate when the message came in that put him on the fast track to Singapore. He told the night clerk that he'd lost the key to 203, and without further question, the clerk gave him the key to Jack's room. The first clue was there, the package wrapped in brown paper...the trophy, his friend had called it. Very carefully, he slit the paper so he could wrap it again. "Wow, nice trophy." He looked at the signature and the date and realized that his buddy must have painted this gal years ago. "So now, I've got to age a face as well as decipher a hiding place somewhere in a mega city." He spotted several band-aids on the dresser and used them to re-tape the painting. Then he and the painting took a taxi to the airport where they caught the next flight to Singapore. As he passed through the check-in areas, he watched the news along with the rest of the world. He was silent and stoic waiting to board the aircraft, giving no hint of the rush of adrenaline coursing inside him, "The bastards... the damn so-called heaven seeking sons of bitches."

He spent his time in the air going over instructions that he'd scribbled on a napkin. He asked the hostess for a double scotch, and as an afterthought, he asked for a Singapore phone book. She not only bought him the drink, much to his surprise she also bought him a phone book. "That beats JAL service all to heck," he joked. Can I buy you a drink?"

"Thanks, but I'm working, she winked teasingly.

He spent the entire trip looking at the napkin, and searching through the phone book. He made a list and reworked it over and over. As soon as the plane landed and he could pass safely though the exits, he was on his way. It wasn't yet dawn. He found a taxi driver who agreed to be a willing partner in this critical scavenger hunt and they went to work on the quest.

There were eight possibles based on his interpretation of Jack's cryptic conversation. The first didn't seem to exist anymore. The second turned out to be a day school with no one on the premises at 5:30 a.m. It was the same for the third. The fourth was apparently not harboring anyone that they wanted to surrender. They weren't even willing to listen. He knocked on the door of the fifth, after several minutes a tiny lady who wasn't overly cordial answered the door. Her stone clad exterior didn't offer him much encouragement, but he went ahead with an inquiry. As soon as Jenk stopped talking, she disappeared back into the recesses of the Center. She didn't completely close the door behind her, so he simply stood and waited.

A committee of three came to the door in a few minutes, the tiny lady, a woman who was most probably a nun... and the 'trophy'. "Bingo," was his first greeting. He flashed a smile of accomplishment. "Excuse me, I'm Jenk Wesley, I think you're expecting me," he looked directly at Gage.

The Sister answered promptly, "Please come right in."

Gage noted quickly that there were eyeballs in both eye sockets... it was a little awkward to stare any closer. As they walked toward the living quarters she informed him that she was supposed to ask a couple of questions.

"Go," he shot back.

"You were sued by a woman. What was her name and what was it for?"

"Thanks, JC, for putting that impressive tidbit of information in circulation," he chuckled. "Her name was Maggie and she was looking for palimony."

"And you're from Georgia, right?"

"And you're pretty good at this, thought you'd throw me a curve, didn't you? Actually, I'm from Wisconsin."

"I'm Gage McClendon, nice to meet you. This is Kwan and this is Sister Esther. We've heard the news. It's difficult to process the scope of the whole disaster."

"I know," Jenk stopped himself from getting into a conversation on it. "Can you get your things, so we can get out of here."

"I just have my purse with me. What's going on? Why did Jack just walk away?"

"He proceeded without answering her, "Sister, could you call a taxi for me? We'll talk later, for now let's concentrate on getting out of Singapore."

Sister Esther generously offered that she and Kwan would take them to the airport.

"This is crazy! I don't want to leave him like this," Gage protested. "Besides, my suitcase is at the hotel."

"We're not going back to the hotel. Look, the guy is nuts about you and wants to make sure you stay safe. I've got instructions to take you home, so for now, just think of me as your bodyguard. Have you got your passport?"

She gave an affirmative nod.

Kwan drove around to a side door and they climbed into an old Ford van. The woman's diminutive stature took on a different aspect behind a steering wheel. She could have easily power driven an eighteen wheeler. Sister Esther Concetta didn't talk much on the way to the airport, but in her silence, she gave the impression that she was well aware of the gravity of international terrorism. Jenk tried to be reassuring at the confusion Gage had to be feeling at this moment. All the while Kwan bulldozed her way through lane changes and off ramps. Jenk cautioned that speed really wasn't the first consideration… getting there alive was the priority.

Kwan delivered her passengers as close as she could to the terminal and they said their goodbys. Gage couldn't help but think about the flight into Singapore and the enormous contrast between her emotions then and now. The airport was bathed in a spiritual solemnity and people were standing in quiet clusters around the televison monitors. Jenk insisted that Gage stay at his side. She accompanied him to a locker area where he retrieved his flight bag and the kraft paper wrapped package. And she was at his side when he got their tickets and checked the items through. The wait for the flight would be about an hour and a half unless the stateside airports were ordered to stay closed longer than the initial mandatory closing following the attack. They walked to a vending machine and got a cup of coffee and then sat down where they could visit.

Jenk started the conversation, "I know you've got lots of questions, and you should... but I'm not going to have all the answers for you. There are some things I can tell you, and some things I can't, and there are a lot of things that I don't know." He looked at her when he talked and saw a striking face that radiated an inner beauty, not to mention a pretty neat body. "I see why Callahan wants you under lock and key. Meeting up with you in the states really put him in a tailspin. He doesn't get shook very often, but when he thought he might miss his plane due to a situation on an island the morning he was to meet up with you here... well, that shook him up big time!"

"You know I'm in love with him," Gage volunteered.

"I'd say it's written on all over you," he acknowledged. "What I don't understand is, how he painted a picture of you over thirty years ago that looks exactly like you today." The former Navy pilot was stringing out his dialogue with her in order to steer away from issues that he didn't want to get into at this moment.

"You've seen the painting? He told me about it and how he painted the way things would eventually look."

"I've not only seen it, I just checked it through baggage. It was an order from your guy. He got it right, it could have been painted yesterday."

"I'm anxious to see it, but I still don't want to go home without him."

"Sorry gal, but we're going without him." He laughed, "you're going on your own feet or slung over my shoulder, your choice."

Gage observed that both Jack and Jenk had the same matter-of-fact dispositions, even their mannerisms were similar. Both swirled their coffee round and round constantly in the cup. Both looked straight at you when they talked, but you had the feeling that they were seeing a whole lot more than just you. "So I could go back like bagged game, a trophy, huh? I heard him mention the word 'trophy'. That brings me to another point. I listened to his conversation with you, how could you possibly find us in a city teeming with people and with no more instructions than he gave you?"

"A lot of years of solving riddles."

"Why did he have to disguise what he was saying….pick up your party at the school of little fishers or something."

"Little fish eaters," Jenk corrected her and gave a limited explanation. "Trophy… well, you heard him describe the trophy and where it was, and I found it in his room wrapped in brown paper just as he said. Knew from the subject matter that I was looking for an attractive round-eyed woman. Also knew that she would be at a school… little fisheaters had to be Catholic children. Comprehend?"

"Yea, it's incredible. But it still doesn't tell me why he had to be so cryptic." She threw her hands in the air, "and you're not going to tell me, are you? Just tell me this… is he in some kind of danger?"

"Everything is potentially dangerous right now. A plane trip could be dangerous. A football stadium full of people could be dangerous. Anything that would get these loonies a little notoriety is a possible target."

"Jesus, he's involved in some covert way, isn't he?"

She tried to chisel deeper into semantics while Jenk stayed wisely glued to the television.

It was another two and a half hours before they were allowed to board the plane and during that time Changi Airport remained eerily silent. The boarding process had mottled overtones of sadness and fear. The pair slipped quietly into their seats. Jenk, in the role of escort and protector, put Gage at the window seat solidly locked in by his brawny frame. The return flight seemed like an eternity. A splendid assortment of movies didn't seem to hold the travelers attention. There was a lot of tension, even a pervasive mood of suspicion. She tried to pry information out of Jenk. He promised once again that he would tell her what he could, but that this was not the time nor the place.

He tried to change the subject. "Tell me more about you? I'm gonna live with you, gal, and I don't have a clue what you're all about."

She looked at him. He was smiling, and at this point she felt grateful to have his company. "Where do you want me to begin, childhood, single years, marriage, or what?"

"Don't care much for childhood, let's start with the single years. Better yet, tell me how you met JC."

The words spilled out. She talked about the handsome pilot, the risky missions, the decimation of an obscure country, and the politics behind the so-called 'Conflict'. Jenk eased down in his seat, he had her in a comfort zone now. She talked and he listened. At one point, she realized his intent and called him on her relaxed feeling, "Okay, I see what you did, Mr. Psychologist. You didn't want to hear about Jack, you just wanted to get me away from the questions. Well, it worked… I almost forgot for a moment that I haven't a clue why you and I are together on this flight." She added, "not that there's anything wrong with you, but I went to Singapore to meet one guy and came home with another. I can't imagine how this will play in my office." She smiled thinking of Frank… he would really freak out on this scenario.

"There, keep smiling… just like that. You've got a great smile. And the rest of you looks pretty well put together too." He saw a brief look of apprehension and added, "Put your mind at ease, I tease a lot but I'd never cross the line. Callahan is the best friend that I have in the world."

Gage touched his arm, "Thanks, I appreciate that."

"But when we get to Chicago… because I'm traveling real light, you've got to go shopping with me for shorts and socks and shaving cream. I'm supposed to keep you with me, remember?"

"You're kidding, it's that chancy? Is it because I could be an avenue to him?"

"It's because I was told to watch over you, and I take my buddy's requests seriously."

She braced herself against the seat, " I can't believe what my life has come to!"

"What, you mean you don't always travel with a bodyguard? Are you a card player?" He doubted that she was, but he was going to have to find some base on which to build some common interests or he was afraid the close proximity might start irritating her. One of the reasons he'd stayed unmarried was that he never cared much to share his interests. This might prove to be the most difficult assignment that he'd ever had. Although, a hasty glance at the gal sitting next to him made him feel more prone to sharing than say with Maggie, or Sarah, or even Lily…and he'd come real close with Lily. He rested his head on the seat and thought about the wanderlust that had been dragging him around all his life. The next awareness he had was that of a soft hand pushing a pillow under his head. "Thanks," he moved to position himself. "I think I dozed in the middle of a conversation. Sorry."

"It's okay. You sleep and I'll watch… for whatever," Gage replied tongue in cheek.

"Not a bad deal, not a damn bad deal," he slurred as he sank into the first sleep he had since the night before last in Jakarta. It was a deep sleep, not the light sleep where he frequently dreamed he was streaking across the enemy skies in his sleek Navy fighter. In fact, the next sound that pierced his comatose world was the sound of the 'fasten your seatbelt' bell and the nudge of his seat buddy.

"Los Angeles coming up, Jenk," she whispered, so as not to shock him awake too rapidly.

25

    This time he was concerned... concerned that his focus wasn't as sharp as it needed to be at this crucial point. His personal life in order for once, but the mission wasn't the entire focus of his mental acuity. Jack Callahan knew all too well the danger of less than total focus. He'd seen the results too often. Operatives who weren't focused were easy targets. As he slithered along the dark streets, he opted to put a new goal in place. He always had the goal of a successful mission... but this time he was ready to couple it with... the last mission. He was ready to leave the shadowy covert world behind. He'd retired once and the Agency enticed him back to work on a contract basis.

    Although, he'd traveled without incident in and out of Kabul and Jalalabad in the last couple of years, it was never far from his mind that there was an al-Qaeda contract out on him. Tonight it was front and center in his thinking as he made his way to the spectral nether world beneath an abandoned warehouse in Singapore's Chinatown.

    Some years ago the CIA had asked him to collect information on the Afghanistan based international terrorist cells. Now his job was to direct other operatives in infiltrating the al-Qaeda compounds. It wasn't a job that he took on lightly. It was carried out in dirty, putrid surroundings and was like living with a knife at your back all the time. The last phone call that he took from the Agency before he left the Children's Center would probably be the last word that he would hear from them until he finished the mission. You couldn't chance being tapped. It was a lonely and frightening path and any agent who claimed otherwise was in denial. At times, you were even afraid to dream, afraid you would give something away that would blow your cover.

    But those were the negatives. Fanatics, driven by hate, couldn't be allowed to annihilate at will, the rest of the world. And this gave purpose to his staying with the Agency . If indeed, this was the work of the Taliban, or al-Qaeda terrorists, and even this early it looked like their style, this time they'd pushed the buttons of every sane being in the universe, and it was open season on them and their sympathizers.

    A drunk staggered toward him, everyone and everything was suspect at this time. It fostered a further oblique route to his destination. There was nothing easy in this business, often the pitch black night was the only friend you'd have.

When the time was right, he entered the cellar. It was well hidden and superbly disguised. Thankfully, it was still safe. Two agents were quietly studying maps. Both were field people with terrorism experience, but neither of them had ever worked the al-Qaeda network. Jack guessed that the CIA would probably use between fifty to seventy five operatives and it would be up to him to supply the intelligence information to accomplish a common goal, that of bringing down the Taliban and obliterating the al-Qaeda terrorist cells.

There was no time to wonder whether Jenk interpreted the fishing message. There was profound trust in the capability of his friend . JC knew he was looking at weeks if not months of long hours of deep concentration on maps and habits and position coordinates of the enemy. Dim lighting and mealy food were the perks of the job. Days and nights would soon become indistinguishable as the agents locked into a tunnel rat mode.

It was extremely close work and close living and most of the operatives were A type personalities. The strain on their psyches was powerful and as always happened in situations like this, stress routinely sapped their vitality. It was when they began to edge into throes of paranoia, that they'd have to pull back a little. Then decks of cards would appear, and they'd get lost in poker games or black jack for a couple of days. Interesting, how the camaraderie of card games can bring back one's perspective and momentum.

Although Singapore was, by international standards a mellow city, the al-Qaeda moiled like cancer deep in its bowels. It was in this underworld where Callahan first learned he was on an al-Qaeda hit list. It had to do with intelligence gathered on chemical and biological weapons, code named Zabadi, Arabic for 'curdled milk'. He'd spent some frightful months covertly collecting and deciphering data on that ascription. It was evidently critical enough to earn him a slot on the hit list. For Jack, having a contract out on him meant he'd gotten to them real good. And getting to them real good was what it was all about.

26

The domestic flights were back in the air and Gage and Jenk took an uneasy flight form Los Angeles back to Chicago. Uneasy, because it was not the relaxed air time that one was accustomed to, it was a tense, and severely depressed group of passengers. She tried thinking about the Gallery. The show that she'd scheduled next... somehow it didn't seem appropriate now. Too dark... too morbid, she needed to reschedule it.

"You, okay?" Jenk asked as they waited for the 'trophy' painting to come along on the carousel. "You're sure quiet."

"Yea, I'm fine, just thinking about rescheduling the next exhibit I've got lined up. If you were coming to a show right now, would you want to see paintings... good paintings mind you, but paintings that represent deep, dark, psychotic dreams? Or would you want to see light and playful works....or is that the wrong approach to the seriousness of the Twin Towers disasters?"

"You're asking a jet jockey? Honey, you've reached the bottom of the evolution chain for art appreciation when you're asking me about paintings. I know Mona Lisa and Whistler's Mother. But, something playful sounds a hell of a lot better than psychotic dreams even under the best of conditions, I'd say."

"That's a valid opinion. Uh oh, here I come, or rather the painting comes on the carousel, right? How did you get it boxed if it was just wrapped in brown paper. And when do I get to see it?"

"Singapore Airport can do anything, they've got the best customer service in the world... and they do everything with a smile. You don't get to see it until JC shows it to you and I don't want to see any traces of attempted pilfering," he tapped her shoulder for added emphasis.

They took a taxi from the airport. Jenk did a quick perusal of the driver exactly as Jack had done in Singapore... this driver passed scrutiny and they headed for downtown Chicago. It was an odd couple indeed...never, ever could she have anticipated this moment. McClendon and bodyguard, it was almost comical if the situation surrounding it hadn't been so disastrous. Luckily, his humor came across in a very uninhibited way. If you have to take home a guy you don't know, you might as well take home a good-natured one, she told herself.

No sooner had they gotten to the apartment door than Mrs. Giovanni spotted them and came running with outstretched arms. "Honey, honey, I'm so glad you're back. What a terrible disaster!!! I was afraid that they might not let you back in the country."

"Why? She didn't do anything," Jenk quipped.

At that, Mrs. Giovanni stepped back and gave him a royal once over. "Your boyfriend?" she looked at Gage whimsically.

"No actually, he's not. He's a friend of my friend, and he's going to stay with me until my friend comes back to the states. Could be awhile. How are you, Mrs. Giovanni?"

Mrs. Giovanni didn't hear the question, she was too busy trying to unravel the friend of a friend part of the conversation. She walked away still puzzling it out loud.

"Oh this is going to be interesting," Gage realized. "Your room is on the right," she said pointing down the hall. "Make yourself at home, I've got to make some phone calls. Oh, and the coffee is in the upper cabinet next to the stove. I don't have any beer." She was assuming he was a beer drinker, he looked like one, whatever that meant.

"Don't forget, we've got to go shopping."

"My god, you sound like a husband," she said laughing.

She picked up the phone, Greta first, Frank next. Greta was so elated to hear from her friend that Gage could hardly squeeze in a word. Greta gave an almost hysterical report of the New York tragedy...then a blow by blow account of the shortcomings of Mike's new woman, and finally, "I'm sorry, I haven't asked one word about your trip. I can't wait to hear everything. Most importantly, did he come back with you?"

"No, he couldn't come, he sent a substitute."

There was quiet. And then a slow, "Lord, are you kidding?"

"Well, that's simplifying it somewhat. Jack is working in some aspect of this whole international thing. He wanted to make sure I got back safely, so he sent a friend of his to look after me. He's staying with me until further notice, I guess." She tried to give an abridged version of events but Greta had to have details, so the conversation continued on for another thirty minutes. Finally, "Look, we'll talk more at work tomorrow."

Gage hurried to the kitchen where Jenk was finishing a cup of coffee and they set off on a shopping trip for shorts and socks and shaving cream. The amiable visitor turned out to be a dream to shop with... he was patient and he had good shopping skills as well as good taste. They spent a couple of hours buying him a new wardrobe. On the way home, they talked a little about how involved he was going to be in her life. It was going to be more than she wanted, but he was unwavering, so she let it go.

"You're not going to work with me, I hope. I can guarantee my boss wouldn't be thrilled with that," she apprised him before he could give any cause why he should go with her.

"Tell you what, I'll accompany you every morning and be there every evening when you leave the building, how's that?"

"Do I have any choice?" she reacted in exasperation.

"Not really," Jenk smiled. "Be patient and tomorrow sometime I'll try and fill in some of the gaps for you. You've been a good sport, and that makes my job much easier. If you don't mind, I'm going to use my new bedroom and hit the sack." He walked toward the hall and turned back. "Do me a favor, will you? Promise me you won't do anything to put my job on the line… like going out after I go to bed."

"Yes dad," she answered with childlike expressiveness. "Seriously, I don't want to complicate anything, and I'm pretty easy to get along with. You can relax. Incidently, I have to be at work at eight-thirty."

"I'll be ready."

"Goodnight," Gage called out. "I'm going to turn in too, after I call Frank."

"Whoa," he backed out into the hall again. "Who's Frank? I didn't come over here to watch over my buddy's girl only to have another guy in the mix." He sounded earnest.

"Frank's my best friend. You'll meet him, most mornings I have coffee with him. Don't worry, we're friends….just friends." She realized that this arrangement was definitely going to take a little getting used to. "You'll like him… he can introduce you to some 'chicks'." There was no further response from his room, so she presumed he was already asleep.

She dialed. The pleasingly familiar voice of her friend came on the line.

"Gage," he yelled. "I've been worried to death about you. I know the flight back had to be frightening for you. Wanna talk about it?"

"Sure, if you've got time."

Frank assured her that he had all the time in the world for her. Besides, he wanted to hear the rest of the story, as it were. He grabbed a Bud Light and a bowl of pretzels as he got horizontal on the sofa.

"Sorry to have caused you some worry, but I guess I wasn't as uncomfortable as if I'd have been if I'd been coming back by myself."

He lifted himself up to a sitting position, "Did what's-his-name come back with you?"

"No, what's-his-name didn't, but his friend did. And I can't talk too loud, cause he's already asleep," she couldn't help but peak his attention. It worked, Frank's voice grew higher in pitch.

"Gage baby, you're beginning to enjoy shocking me, aren't you?"

She thought about what he said for a moment. Could be that she did enjoy rankling Frank's spurious sense of propriety. "Jack had to leave shortly after the terrorist attacks, and he sent me back with his buddy."

"Just a wee bit strange, isn't it?" Frank goaded. "How much do you really know about your lover or for that matter, whoever came back with you?"

"It's okay, Frank. We'll talk tomorrow. Wanna meet for coffee before work? My friend... well, my bodyguard," she laughed, "will be with me. You'll like him, he was a Navy pilot."

"Okay, " he chided indignantly. "Alright, bring on the bodyguard, I'll find out what the son-of-a-bitch is up to."

She made him promise to be decent to Jenk. Frank could be a real jerk when he set his mind to it. However, it was too late in the evening to worry about Frank's territorial attitude and as she tiptoed toward her bedroom she could feel the presence of another being. It wasn't intrusive. But it did evoke sensory stimuli, some kind of nostalgia, from somewhere in her memory.

"Good night, Miss McClendon."

The voice metamorphosing through the door surprised her. She answered quietly, "thought you were asleep."

"When you are," his words floated along the hall. He waited patiently until he was sure.

27

The next morning was interesting. Gage, unaccustomed to modesty in her apartment, had to do some quick shuffling as decorous lapses occurred. If Jenk witnessed any erratum, he kept it to himself.

"Jenk, don't make coffee," she called from her room. "We're meeting Frank for coffee before I go to work. I want you to meet my friend."

"I know and I'm not making coffee, I'm just waiting."

"Oh... you were listening to my conversation last night!"

"You weren't whispering... that guy, Frank... does he have a thing for you?"

"Nah, that's just Frank, his macho libido comes into play sometimes," she explained. She didn't exactly know what she meant by those remarks, but she thought that probably a Navy fighter pilot wouldn't either. He didn't question her further and they set out for Anzio's. "Here, wanna drive?" She tossed him the car keys. Traffic was relatively light and with Jenk following directions handily they reached the coffee shop ahead of Frank. In fact, she began to wonder if Frank had misunderstood, when suddenly, she saw him sail through the door.

He glanced at Jenk and then with obvious Beccaccio showmanship lifted Gage off her feet and planted a kiss solidly on her lips and then another on her forehead. He would have kept up the spirit of the moment a little longer, but he caught a stern look of disapproval in her eyes. "I've missed you, girl," he was playing to an audience of one. "Let me get my coffee and I'll introduce myself to your companion."

By the time Frank returned to the table, his behavior had calmed and he was quite pleasant to the stranger sitting close to his best friend. If truth were known, he was probably a little intimidated by the appellation, Navy fighter pilot. He had enough true life experience to be in awe of the 'guts and glory' flying done from the carriers by these larger than life images.

Gage introduced the two. Jenk gave Frank a healthy handshake as she told of Frank's photo journalism days of Vietnam. The two struck up a lively conversation punctuated with obscure oriental phrases and after a few minutes, Frank seemed to forget the task he'd taken on, that of interrogating the escort, and he settled into the role of polished conversationalist. Jenk was good natured and without saying much, he'd managed to win Frank's approval. Gage watched, intrigued by something both Jack and Jenk seemed built on....a quiet confidence that seemed to channel tranquillity to those around them. The words sang-froid came to mind, and Frank was experiencing it firsthand. "Guys, I've got to get to work. You two can sit here and talk."

"I'll walk over with you. I'd like to see the layout of the gallery," Jenk said getting up with the cup of coffee in his hand.

"Look, you can walk to the door with me, but you'll have to give me time to explain some of this to my co-workers. If you want to come back at five-thirty, I'll have things where they'll have a little understanding of your role in my life. And don't forget, we have to talk... tonight!!"

"Gotcha pretty lady, it's just up to the door, then. Nice meeting you, Frank. I'd like to see some of your work."

That got Frank, he loved showing his photos. He didn't even seem to mind the two walking away from him. He got a caffeine refill and started his morning agenda.

"Can I come inside the building this evening, or are you going to make me wait outside?" Jenk asked coyly.

Gage turned to him as they walked up the gallery steps, "You can come in. Nelson, the doorman will show you where to find me." At that moment Nelson came hurrying toward them and gave her a big, hearty hug. She introduced him to Jenk and walked away, back to the routine of shows and openings and all other associated periphery of the art world. Glancing over her shoulder, she saw the two talking together. As they shook hands, she saw Jenk hand Nelson a card, or something about the size of a card. Her quick assessment of Jenk was that he was a handsome guy, even with a blind eye, which was virtually undetectable. He told her he'd never married, yet he seemed to enjoy female company and he was heads above anything she'd seen in the dating scene. She had to know more about his life.

It was chaos for a few minutes in the gallery. Everyone came to welcome her, and truthfully, she was glad to get back to a place where she could concentrate on tangibles she could organize and schedule. Even the reticent Mr. Espinosa made a 'glad to have you back' overture. The first time she and Greta managed some time alone, she questioned Greta on the status of the next exhibit and whether anything had been done to lock it in while she was gone. Greta looked pained that Gage hadn't launched into a full blown account of her jaunt, but answered her question. "No, not yet. We have some time, so we were waiting on you."

"Good, I want to switch it around. It's heavier than I think we should go with on the next one. I've got to get permission to get something lighter in here. I've got an idea." She went on to tell Greta all about Santa Fe, his merits and his eccentricities.

"Sounds good to me, want me to get the Board together, or set up a conference call or something?"

"Whatever works for everybody. I guess, I do need to do it quickly." She could read Greta's face, so she stopped long enough to fill her in a little more on the Singapore saga, the good times… the fabulous guy, even the commitment they'd made in their relationship. When Greta pressed her on whether this meant marriage or moving away, she confessed that the disasters occurred before they'd had much of a chance to do any planning. "Is your life getting any better?" she inquired of Greta.

"Well, now that I'm a single woman with two pre-teen boys to raise, I imagine my life is not going to be my life for a few years yet. But what the heck, they're healthy and we're together. Yea, I'd have to say it's better… more settled for sure."

With that, they got to work. Greta scheduled a couple layers of conference calls and they got a quorum to go along with inviting Santa Fe, sight unseen and solely on Gage's judgement to open a show in Chicago on November 5th, just a little over seven weeks from now. Next hurdle, confronting the orderly world of the artist with a fast paced project that was sure to turn orderliness upside down and backwards. The trump card would be to convince him that this was what Mac would want for him.

The remainder of the day, they worked diligently on the stack of mail cluttering Gage's desk. Until, a knock interrupted their pattern and a grinning Jenk appeared in the doorway, they had no inkling of time. "You did say five-thirty, right?" he asked politely.

She assured him that he'd heard right, and taking his arm she introduced him to Greta, "My right arm," she said of her assistant, "Jenk, this is Greta, and Greta meet Jenk. Greta would you mind showing Jenk what we do here… or at least, show him the galleries… and I'll finish this letter for Mr. Espinosa." She worked on as the pair took a quick tour of the place. She heard Greta telling Jenk that she was going to hold him personally responsible if anything happened to her friend. They were too far away for her to hear his answer. She finished her writing about the time they wandered back her way.

"What do you think of the galleries?" Gage asked.

Before he could answer, Greta piped up, "I think he was more interested in door openings and closets, and what was behind draped surfaces than art."

'Was not," he allayed. "I'm impressed. Maybe a little culture will attach itself to me."

She closed down the computer, told Greta good night, and they headed out. This was the first time all day that she'd had time to think about Jack. The closeness that was happening between her and Jenk made her miss all the more what she should be having with the guy she left behind in Singapore. She corrected her thought, the guy who left her behind in Singapore.

"Surprise," Jenk called out as they entered the apartment, "dinner is served, Madame."

"Holy cow, I smell spaghetti!"

"Close, it's lasagna," he responded with an pseudo Italian accent. "If I'm going to be hanging around here, I've got to help out some. My mom didn't raise no slacker. I hope you don't mind my puttering around."

Gage was delighted. "You had to have shopped, I didn't have any lasagna pasta. And you got bread too… and chianti! Okay right now, tell me, why are you single? Are you gay?"

"Now what the hell makes you ask that?"

"You're not married, you ought to be married. You'd be a great husband," she said apologetically. "You're thoughtful, you're handsome and you have a sense of humor," she added.

"I just never found my 'Gage'. Do you know I'm really a cyclops, I only have one eye."

She told him with the story of JC telling her to look for a guy with one eye, but she didn't know whether he meant blind or with the whole eyeball missing. They ate and drank wine and generally had a grand evening. Even cleaning up the dishes was cordial and pleasant. Gage thanked him once again for the meal and he warned her that it wouldn't happen every night.

"Okay, I know you're chomping at the bit to hear anything I can tell you. Wait til' I get my props," he said walking to the bedroom. He returned with a deck of cards. "I can talk better if I've got a game going. Come to think of it, that may be another reason I'm not married. Who wants to talk to a guy who talks with a deck of cards in his hands all the time."

"If the right woman came along, the cards would probably be needing a new home."

"That's a kind thing to say. I don't know though, I like my cards, my booze, and anything going over a hundred and fifty miles an hour, especially if it has a cockpit and wings."

"Alright, enough stalling."

"Whew, stall, that's in my vocabulary."

"Jenk, come on. Where is Jack and what's going on?"

He started a slow shuffle and a methodical game of solitaire. "Callahan and I go way back. He was Air Force and I was Navy and when we retired, neither of us could give up the adrenaline rush, the almost not making it, that made making it, so alluring... and we were both super patriotic. I was from a farm in Wisconsin and he was off a Wyoming ranch." He went on to tell her how they'd both put out feelers to find something connected with flying, something that would be adventurous, and something where they could still be of service to their country. "To make a long story short, we were recruited separately by the Agency and put together as a team, and lo and behold...here we are, still together after all these years," he said pretending to play a violin. He saw a deep furrow form on her forehead. "Is that a problem, Callahan and myself, a team?"

"No, but.... Agency, is that another way of saying CIA? Oh my god, don't tell me he's really CIA covert in a hostile country, don't tell me that, please don't tell me that!"

Still playing a slow game of solitaire, he went on, as if deaf to her pleading. "Look, he's a senior officer, he's calling the shots, not taking them. Your man is smart, he doesn't make mistakes. I don't know exactly where he is, it's a big and complicated area that he's collected intelligence on over the last few years." He finished the solitaire game, showing her that he won. He wasn't going to tell her much more, no matter how hard she tried to wheedle information out of him. Except for one thing, he had to make her aware of the gravity of her safety. He stopped shuffling the cards and laid the deck on the table face down. "There's one more point, I've got to get across to you... and you've got to absorb it one hundred percent. Jack's expertise is a real threat to the lunatic terrorists he's been tracking. They know of him and about him, what we don't know is... how much they know about him. It's a long shot, but they could have been shadowing him in Singapore. Supposing they were aware of his presence there, that's why we didn't go back to the hotel and that's why the cryptic phone call. I don't think there's a motherfuckin' chance in hell that they're aware of his path, but you don't ever want to underestimate the enemy. All I ask of you is that you let me do my job, and that is, making sure that you're safe until Prince Charming comes home. Hey, look, I bought some beer today, want one?"

"Sure," the words sort of tumbled out as if out of a robot. She touched her head, perspiration was beaded up all over. For a moment, she thought she was going to faint. Jenk saw the limpness as she drew her hand across her face. He grabbed a towel, wetting it with the cold beer he'd just gotten out of the refrigerator.

"Sweetheart, I promise you're going to be safe."

"It's him, promise me he's gonna be safe, can you? Dammit! Can you?"

"No, I can't. Right now, if he was in a poker game, I'd say he'd have to have at least a straight flush to win and probably a ten high straight flush at that."

"Is that the ultimate hand?" Gage fumbled for words.

"Nope, there's the ace high royal flush, but that's pretty dang rare. Look, our boy is involved in a high stakes poker game of sorts, but remember this... he is one hell of a world class player."

The aviator shuffled the deck of cards and insisted that she get her mind off their discussion by playing a couple of poker hands. "I'm not very educated in the art field, but before Callahan comes back I can make a real poker hustler out of you."

"Just what he'd want I'm sure." She had to brighten up, Jenk wasn't going to let her stay maudlin very long. She reached out and picked up the cards.

"Okay, gal, let's do a little traveling, some international poker games, English Stud, Canadian Five Card, and Curaçao Stud. How about a little of each of those games?"

There was no way to say no to the guy. He was so pleasant and upbeat that before she could answer, she found herself involved in the history of Curaçao Stud, a popular poker game in the Netherlands and Dutch West Indies. Poker sessions became the beginning of a pattern of waiting... later on, Frank became a regular and once in a while Greta dropped by. In fact, Greta's lack of concentration from trying to keep up with the arrangements for getting her boys back and forth to their various sports, prompted Mr. Navy to offer to take over some of the afternoon chauffeuring duties. He insisted rather humorously that he needed another wifely chore to go along with waiting on the opposite sex and cooking. He failed to mention that he couldn't bear to miss an opportunity to get as many hands into a game as possible. In fact, Mrs. Giovanni's name was brought up as a possible player, prompting Gage's quick axing of the notion. From her Old Maid cards level of skill, to throwing out terms like belly-buster straight... fifth street... and cinch hand, Gage was a good sport in the ongoing waiting game... and the waiting was, indeed, less lonely thanks to Jenk's longtime love affair with a deck of cards.

28

It took two weeks of long and repetitive phone conversations to feel confident in Santa Fe's understanding of his upcoming exhibit. Gage promised to send a couple of gallery people and a Ryder truck to pack and haul the art work to Chicago. All she asked of Santa Fe was that he do a brief synopsis of each piece, if possible, and that he be available for the opening. It seemed simple enough, but true to form, nothing was simple that involved Santa Fe. The questions that he should have asked last, he asked first... like how do you get to the gallery. One Friday afternoon after one such exhausting conversation, she looked up to see Frank standing in the doorway with his camera lens zeroed in on her.

"Oh Frank, I'm so glad to see you," she exclaimed. "Quick, say something to me I can understand the first time you say it."

"That bad, huh? Was that your friend? I heard some of the conversation. Ought to be a trip meeting him."

"Trip is right, you can't imagine. Hey, what brings you downtown."

He paused a second, "Well, I never get to see you without your shadow, not that he's objectionable or anything, but I just wanted to see how you're really doing. Have you heard anything at all?"

"No, not a word. If Jenk knows anything, he's not talking. But I don't think he'd be staying if he thought Jack wouldn't be coming back. There wouldn't be a reason."

He tilted her chin and then changed the shutter speed. "I haven't done any shots of you in a long time, head back, please. Okay, hold it... great! Could he be staying, because of you?"

"No," she responded adamantly. "Actually, he questioned me about my relationship with you."

"It's a territorial thing, my dear. Are we playing cards tonight?"

"Don't you have a date, Frank?. It's Friday night."

He indicated that he needed to lay low awhile. A spunky young gal who'd hired him to do a modeling folio had dropped anchor on his doorstep and he was beginning to feel a little hemmed in. Frank couldn't seem to handle a relationship that went beyond casual... or casual sex. He was really running from this gal... enough to volunteer to bring all booze and food to insure there would be a poker table. "I miss you, girl. Never thought I'd have to share you with a couple of cavalier pilots. As a matter of fact, I guess it never entered my thoughts that I'd ever have to share you with anybody," he whimpered half joking.

"Come on, guy… you're still my best friend."

"Remember it! Cards tonight?"

"Sure thing," Gage assured him as he tucked the camera back into a shoulder sling and scooted out the door. "Wanna play cards tonight?" She called to Greta who was deep in concentration unraveling the chronology of Santa Fe's life and career.

"I guess, or I should say, if I can get my mind back on track. Are you aware that either this guy went to college before he was born or he's got some dyslexic facts on the bio sheet that he faxed up here? And he couldn't decide if he did or if he didn't serve in the Army. You're right, meeting him ought to be a real trip. And get this…he says he'll go take some of his paintings off of the walls of people who own them. It sounds like he'd just walk in and take them away."

"Doesn't surprise me. It sounds exactly like what he'd do." Gage smiled. Was Chicago ready for this explosion of irrational rationale? She felt confident that the timing was right for this show. Personally, right now Santa Fe gave her a point of concentration that kept her sane in a no questions-no answers environment.

"Your ride's here," Greta sung out as Jenk walked through the door.

No need to hurry, there was usually a ten minute discussion of sports topics between the single mom and the shuttle service guy, so Gage finished working out an agenda for tomorrow's board meeting. Before long, Jenk took her jacket off the coat rack and held it as she slid her arms into the sleeves. Their evening walk toward the exit was now a familiar pattern around the gallery, so much so that he was openly and affectionately addressed as 'bodyguard'.

Every evening she asked the same question, "Have you heard anything at all?"

"I hate like heck to tell you no all the time, but communication is not the nature of this business." He tried to soften it somewhat. "There's a quaint little English pub not far from here that I spotted today, wanna stop for fish and chips and a dark brew."

"When Frank was in this afternoon, I promised him we'd play cards tonight."

"We don't have to spend the evening out, but I was busy driving boys to their after school games and didn't cook," he apologized good-naturedly.

"What, you're not super mom?" she teased. "Let's go for the fish and chips."

"Does Frank come to see you often?" He knew she'd said that he was just a friend, but in Jenk's thinking....just friends was strange relationship between a handsome man and a sensual gal who seemed to enjoy each other's company. "Was there ever anything between you two, and why not?"

"Yes, he does come to see me often. He does the photos for the exhibit promos, so sometimes it's a professional visit, other times it's just social. She thought for a second as to whether she should offer further explanation, then decided to go ahead, "No, there was never anything between us... not the right chemistry I guess... certainly not the Callahan 'stop me dead in my tracks' chemistry. Anything else, sir?"

"That'll do... right answer. Gotta look out for my pal."

They drove to the little pub that looked almost authentic with its wattle and daub facade. The waitress was, without a doubt, very authentic. She was a Brit from Suffolk County, East Anglia. Years ago Jenk flew in and out of Bentwaters Air Base a number of times and so the two carried on a long conversation about the legend of the ghost pilot that supposedly appeared in night shadows along the runway from time to time. Her name was Sheila and she could hardly do enough for them after that. Their fish and chips came super sized. "Enjoy... this is some of the best cod in the world, flown in fresh, never frozen," she was all but giddy in her kudos to the fare.

They dug into the golden battered mounds of cod until gluttony brought them to stoppage. Jenk ordered each of them a dark beer and they sat quietly chatting for awhile. Gage couldn't hear enough about Jack. She tried once again to pry into this particular assignment, and failing, settled for details of his life. Finally, in mock exasperation, Jenk raised both hands in the air, "Okay, let me tell you a story about JC... maybe, you can see his character, his competitive nature."

He began with Madame Nyugen. "Madame Nyugen was a frail but fiery little lady, of French and Vietnamese ancestry and she despised the Vietcong. She was a dukes mixture of fortuneteller, soothsayer, and pharmacist. Apparently, Jack became friends with her in Nam when he stopped at her hut to see if any of her aromatics would work on a sinus condition. She recognized the patch on his flight suit as that of a dragon man and to her that meant they had a common enemy, the Cong. From there on JC was special, number one G.I. she called him. Callahan listened to her folklore and legends, he must have enjoyed them because he retold them often enough, but mostly I think he felt sorry for her. Supposedly, at one time she enjoyed wealth, her husband had some sort of government position before he was assassinated by a Vietcong hit squad. After that, Madame had to learn a trade to support herself so she turned to oriental mysticism and became quite successful. Callahan never knew whether the legends she related so reverently, came after the fact or whether she had a propensity for mysticism before her husbands death. It didn't matter, he thought enough of her to return to visit with her after every international mission he went out on, even after the Mogadishu ambush."

Gage was startled. "Somalia?"

"In 1993 he'd just gone undercover in Somalia looking for al-Qaeda connections when the ambush occurred. He spent five days trapped under the floorboards of an al-Qaeda hideout. He's never said much about the terror of those five ungodly long days lying under the feet of some of the craziest lunatics in the world."

"Jesus! How did he get out?"

"Don't have a clue, it couldn't have been pretty. He never mentions it and if you bring it up, the only thing he says was that Madame Nyugen's keys kept him alive. Said he couldn't break up a set of keys, and at the time he only had two of the three."

"Two of three... keys?"

"Yep. Seems that while he was in Nam, the little 'snake-oil' widow told him the legend of the three keys. They had to do with initiation and knowledge. The silver key represented passage through psychological understanding, the second key, the gold key, was for philosophical wisdom. Watching over him during his tour in Vietnam, Madame said he'd earned the first two keys and she gave him both the silver and the gold key when he left the country. She told him that through acquisition of the gold and silver key he had the power to act... he was empowered to act in the noblest and highest form of service to his country. To make a long story short, after returning from a visit with Madame Nyugen following Mogadishu, there was a diamond key along with the silver and gold keys on his key chain."

Gage remembered seeing the three keys. Not knowing just what to say to such a colorful vignette of the man she loved, she simply asked, "Would you say the guy loves a challenge?"

"Pretty fair assessment," he agreed as he handed Sheila his credit card.

Gage recalled Jack saying he never bought wine to lay up for the future, he bought wine that someone else had already laid up, because even tomorrow was too far away to count on.

Jenk wasn't surprised and he further added, that because Callahan believed each day was the most important day of his life he thought it his lot to enjoy the best that life could offer. "That puts you in mighty tall company, kid." he chuckled.

She didn't answer, didn't know exactly what to say. Then a bit hesitantly she asked, "Was he in love with Mrs. Nyugen?"

"Hell no, Madame Nyugen was as about as appealing as last years roses. She sincerely cared about him like a son and he found her mysterious and fascinating, and he respected her survival instincts. But, speaking of roses... this past summer in a card game the guys were teasing Jack about having nothing to strive for now that he had all three keys... seems everyone knows the story of Madame Nyugen. The son-of-a-gun laughed and told them they were wrong. Apparently, the little lady had thrown him a higher piece of mysticism to work on... a level of absolute achievement... the symbol, a golden rose. Only this time, she didn't give him a clue... no clue at all as to what absolute achievement meant. According to him, she put her finger to her lips and in a hushed voice told him that one day the wind would speak to him and he would recognize it as absolute achievement, whatever the heck that means. She indicated she wouldn't be there to present him with the rose, it had to be of his own unique character and for his own unique purpose... but, as he became aware of this mysterious absolute achievement... and she guaranteed him that he would achieve it and that he would recognize it, then he could acquire his own golden rose. And that's the Madame Nyugen story, let's go play cards."

"Incredible story," Gage uttered as they walked toward the apartment. She was mulling over the strangeness of it when her thoughts were interrupted by the sight of a bewildered Frank propped against the door of her apartment surrounded by six packs and snack sacks.

He whined a little a being inconvenienced, but it was all forgotten as soon as the cards hit the table. Greta arrived shortly thereafter and the foursome became hopelessly fearful opponents in poker hands laced with ridiculously stupid jokes and just one more beer. But throughout the evening, every time Gage looked at her hand, Madame Nyugen looked back at her from a little hut in a faraway country, so much so that she was glad when the beer was gone and the poker hands began to fumble.

She cleaned up the table while Jenk saw Frank and Greta to their cars. He returned with an apologetic sound in his voice, "I'm sorry, if I gave you more than you wanted with Jack's background."

"I'm glad you did, I worry about him, that's all."

"I know, I do too. Goodnight, luv."

As he started toward his room he heard, "By the way, tomorrow is the one day a month that I volunteer at the homeless shelter."

"Oh, shit," echoed along the hall.

29

"Please! We're beginning to sound like we're married," Gage admonished. "I'm scheduled for work at the shelter today, and I'm going, like it or not."

"I don't like it, and I wish you'd reconsider."

"Sorry, Jenk, but I can't let you completely run my life. It'll be okay. Nobody there even knows what al-Qaeda is, or cares a crap, if that's what you're afraid of. They just want a hot meal and a little TLC."

"Sweetheart, in the words of your guy himself, 'Never ever underestimate your enemy'."

She didn't budge. "You can go with me, if you want, but I am going."

"Okay, Ms. Hardhead, let's roll," he stayed a good sport. She didn't get it, but there was nothing relative to terrorist awareness in this country. It was her right, simple and plain, her right to go where she set her mind. Ninety nine percent of the time, it would be safe. It was that other one percent that concerned him. More than once, he'd seen some of that totally innocent one percent mowed down without second thought or remorse.

The shelter was crowded. A cold snap had driven the street people to look for warmth. The kitchen was a huge cacophony of pots and pans and shrill voices in various dialects. Gage was assigned to the tray line by an ample bosomed matron. When Jenk stepped in to dip the gravy as Gage scooped mashed potatoes, the buxom broad took offense at his acting without orders. "So fire me," he mumbled under his breath, and she almost did. Gage had to interfere, or she would have tossed him into the kitchen with the garbage.

"That will teach you, smart alec," she chided. They kidded and jostled each other as they worked. Gage was kind and gentle and had something to say to each person as she ladled the creamy potatoes onto their plates. After a while, bossy matron warmed to them and she was able to hand the ladle to Jenk and carry a tray for a mother balancing a baby on her hip or an elderly person too crippled to navigate through the jumble of tables and chairs.

It was when he spotted two mid-eastern men coming through the line that Jenk came to attention. His adrenaline zipped out of hibernation as he spotted one of them slide something silver out of his hand and into his pocket.

"Faint, right now, fall like you've fainted," his staccato words came out with force. As he spoke, he pushed her to the floor explaining to the other workers that this always happened when her blood sugar dropped too low. He asked for help getting her to the kitchen where she could get a little orange juice. It happened so quickly that Gage wasn't sure but what she'd really passed out. A burly volunteer rescued her from the floor and carried her into the kitchen. Jenk stayed at his gravy ladle post in surveillance while Gage sat amid the pots and pans sipping a glass of orange juice.

"Clear," he reported as he popped through the swinging doors. "Sorry, I had to do it. A guy coming through the line slid a silver object from his hand into his pocket. Better safe... ."

"Okay Jenk, this is over the edge. My blood sugar? What the hell was that all about?"

"I needed to get you out of the line of fire as fast as possible...blood sugar fainting will take you one down immediately, and be believable. Come on, you can go back to being the mashed potato lady."

They repositioned themselves behind the food bar, Gage still stunned by the events of the last fifteen minutes, and Jenk Wesley acting like nothing had happened.

"Did the guy who caused my sick spell leave?" Gage asked facetiously.

"Nope, he's over there with his friend," he pointed the ladle at two heavily bearded men seated on the far side of the hall. One was taking photos of the other with a sleek silver camera.

"Oh great! My bodyguard fended off the deadly effects of a 35 millimeter camera!"

Jenk had already ascertained that the silver object was a camera. "Say what you want, could have just as well have been something else." It didn't embarrass him and Gage began to see how seriously he took his charge of her safekeeping. She apologized, but he wouldn't let her get too contrite. He held the ladle in the air and let the gravy trickle down into the stainless steel container. "Think we could get carryouts from here, I don't wanna' be in a kitchen again anytime soon."

"My friend, you're a trip... a real trip. Tell you what, for saving my life I'm going to take you to a modern dance revue this evening." It wasn't really like she was treating him to anything, because wherever she went he had to go too. But she'd planned on seeing this highly acclaimed group for sometime and couldn't help that it probably wasn't high on Jenk's list of things to do.

He didn't object, but he suggested that the next time he saved her life, she might try payback in the form of a Chicago Bulls game.

They attended the dance revue as well as a number of other events during the month of October and Jenk was, as always, a willing escort. Gage was grateful to have someone to count on, never more so than each time she watched Greta struggling to balance schedules. Her friend hardly had a chance to go beyond the perimeters of youth sports. "Gret, can I do anything to help you?" Gage asked time and time again.

"No, not really… you know the night we phoned Indonesia all night trying to contact your pilot, that was the most excitement this old gal's had in a long time, " she replied wistfully. "I wish we could do it again, and find him for you."

"Me too, Greta. I'm afraid it's pretty grim. Jenk is on his phone all the time and he never smiles when he's talking. Never says much either, just listens. I honestly don't think he knows where Jack is. Don't tell this, but one day when he was in the shower and his cell phone was on table, I picked it up to check it to check his caller ID. Should have known he clears it after every call."

Greta got up from her desk and came over to Gage, "Do you think you might fall in love with him, Jenk, I mean?"

"Nope, he's a great guy and fun to have as a friend, but no… it's Jack or no one." Suddenly she realized what precipitated the question. "Ah… are you interested in Jenk Wesley, Greta? Well, I do declare," she fanned herself with a file folder and exaggerated her surprise. "Hey, but if you go out with him, I have to go too," she laughed. "Gret, he does have a history of eluding matrimony, you know."

"I don't wanna marry him, it would just be nice to go out with a person of the opposite sex who's over ten years old for once."

She listened to Greta fantasize rather vividly and while they were in the midst of a fit of giggles over some of the more graphic fantasies, the phone rang. The incoherent rambling of Santa Fe immediately dissolved the fanciful mental imagery of their conversation. The next twenty five minutes was spent picking out key words in long disconnected phrases….phrases that wandered aimlessly from topic to topic. By the end of the stroll through muddle and confusion, Gage gleaned what she thought to be a pretty fair assessment of his phone call. He would ride up in the rental truck along with the paintings next week.

From there it was anyone's guess as to what his itinerary would be from arrival until his show.

"Think he plays cards?" Greta quipped.

"Oh, please!!" Then Gage sobered at thoughts of turning him over to a hotel. "My god, I might have to put him on the sofa, the windy city isn't ready for this whirlwind. But, on the other hand, it might be the one thing that might push a handsome Navy pilot to seek safe refuge at my best friend's apartment."

"Welcome to Chicago, Mr. Santa Fe, may you be eccentric to the utmost extreme," gurgled Greta raising her hand in a mock toast.

"Who are we toasting?" Jenk stepped through the doorway, smiling and carrying a pizza box.

Gage coughed and Greta gasped and blushed.

"So, what's going on?" He could tell he'd walked in on some kind of girl talk, and they couldn't tell just how much he'd heard, so a long pause stood between his words and their answers.

Gage was first with, "It could be that we might have another guest at my place next week, the artist of this next show."

"Do you always put up the artists at your apartment?"

"Never, until now," she announced. "But this isn't a normal run of the mill human. This one may be more than your military mind can handle, and... ."

Greta interrupted, "and what have you got in the box?"

"Pizza for the boys. Do you realize that with the make-up game tonight there's barely enough time for you to get home until they have to be at the arena?"

She did, of course, but there wasn't much she could do about it. "Thanks so much, you're a dream," she said taking the pizza. There was a clear and loud cough in the background.

Greta leaned over Gage's desk and with Jenk at her back whispered, "Don't you dare say anything to him!"

Gage gave her the old Girl Scout promise sign and they went through a brief initiation of Santa Fe's eccentricities....just in case he became occupier of the sofa next week. They had Jenk so primed for the preposterous world that was going to descend on him that he was stumped for words. He'd met some looney pilots, surely this wasn't more than they were. Couldn't be more than that crazy son- of-a-bitch 'hoss' McKenzie. He never flew a sober flight. He'd stagger sideways to his plane and grab the oxygen. The brass looked the other way, because his sortie would always be razor sharp. He pushed the plane, himself, and the enemy way beyond normal limits, yet you always knew he was comin' back. If he had a successful mission, he'd hold up a bottle of Jack Daniels immediately after touching down on the carrier. Never once saw him taxi in without that bottle, and never saw anyone spend any time searching for his hiding place. I'm bettin' on 'hoss', he thought to himself.

30

The situation was extremely tense in the Singapore underworld. It was a given that the global web of al-Qaeda cells had networks operating in the area. Among them, the Islamic Liberation Front which was a Filipino group, and the Jamaah Islamiyah, some of whom trained in al-Qaeda camps in Afghanistan. It was the Jamaahs, the Afghan trained terrorists, that occupied most of Jack's days and nights. He'd been on the trail of a couple of their senior operations planners for sometime now, but in order to set up a foolproof dragnet, he needed a good informer. He'd asked the agency time and time again to get him an agent fluent in the language and with a physical profile that could pass for an indigenous operative. He needed a highly skilled decoy to pull in an informant. But each time he asked, he was told that operatives of Mid-eastern ethnicity were virtually non-existent. So, he was forced to get creative.

After a couple weeks of watching the movements of three al-Qaeda suspects, he observed a pattern of behavior that could very possibly exploited. One of the men appeared to have a weakness for other men. He couldn't use a Caucasian for a decoy, that would be suspicious... but he could use one of the two Chinese operatives. After all, they were in Chinatown. One of them, code name Rio, became the CIA's gay man on the street.

Rio hung around on the street corners making tiny overtures, finally striking up whatever kind of conversation a Chinese homosexual and a Islamic terrorist can have together. It didn't take long. In nine days he wove himself into the seamy shadows of Chinatown and into the confidence zone of the enemy. It couldn't have been a smoother set up. In the back seat of an old Mercedes, Rio chloroformed his patsy and delivered him butt naked to the dank cellar operations center. The work to break him down beg an immediately, the first goal being that of identifying the top circle of aides who planned the logistics of attacks. Secondly, they needed to extract the names of bombmakers and paymasters.

For the sake of brevity, they addressed their captive as Opi, based on Rio's understanding that the former occupation of the suspect had been opium trafficking. In the first round of interrogation it was evident that Opi was also a user, it was also clear that he knew a lot, and one way or another they intended to pull it out of him. It actually made it easier that he was an addict, dope could be dangled like a carrot.

Two of the agents had decent Arabic language skills and they grilled the terrorist rigorously, but as the narcotics withdrawal neared Callahan was faced with the dilemma of getting into the drug business. It was easy enough to buy the stuff, and safe if he sent one of the Chinese agents who could blend into the oriental fabric of the area. The tenuous part was that they had to be cautious in using injectable opium. The last time he'd been in a situation where they tried to get information out of a dope head, the agents killed the dopey with a heroin overdose. Jack was convinced that Opi had the data he needed, some of it very high level, so he had to keep the evil son-of-a-bitch alive for now. And he wouldn't be worth shit when the delirium and shakes hit, so Rio was sent to make a buy.

There was a way to insure that they wouldn't lose their guy in shootin' him up. If he could get access to epinephrine, they could bring him up and take him down at will. He hated like hell to involve her, but Sister Esther could probably get him what he needed. It was not only critical to this mission, it was critical to the whole world to squeeze every noxious slimy syllable they could out of the bastard. He waited for the cover of darkness and started a zigzag course toward the Sister's school. He purposely made the trek long, twisting and turning making absolutely certain he wasn't being tailed. Even then he stood totally immobile in the shadows for well over an hour. Involving a civilian was risky, involving an innocent woman, almost unconscionable . He took one last deep breath and headed for the door, hoping trenchantly it wouldn't be Kwan to answer his knock.

"Sister," he said, surprised at her arrival in the doorway. He moved toward the light so she could see him a little better. "Jack Callahan, ma'am, can I come in?"

"Are you sure? I recognize the voice, but not much else. Come on in, I was on my way out to roll up the windows in the van."

It took a moment to register how odd he must look to the nun with his hair and the stubble growth on his face dyed black. "I'm glad you didn't shut the door in my face," he confessed as he scooted into the hallway.

"I take it that the facial hair and the color change is work related."

"Yes, look I've got a huge favor to ask? Is Kwan, or anyone else, around?"

The nun assured him that no one could hear them as she walked with him to her living area. "What do you need, my friend? And, is Gage safely in the Chicago?"

"She's quite safe," he lowered his voice to just above a whisper. "I'm going to be blunt. I need to interrogate someone, and that someone is an opium addict. I wanna' inject him with his drug of choice, but I don't want to kill him. Not yet, anyway. I need to maintain him, keep him needing a fix bad enough to talk....because he has high level information. But, in order to be safe, I've got to have epinephrine to counter the possibility of overshooting him." He had no idea what kind of response he'd get from a person of a religious order. He simply stated his case and waited.

"Mr. Callahan, I think we're both on the same side of justice. I'll help you. I can get epinephrine, but if you're not skilled at using it, you can also overdose, or overshoot as you called it, or even kill a person with it. Have you ever administered it?"

He admitted that he'd never personally done the injections and the only ones he'd ever given were the antibiotic shots he'd helped his dad give cattle when he was a teenager. "I'll manage," he assured her. "But I do need you to get me the epinephrine."

"If you'll let me inject it for you. After all, I am a nurse."

"Look, I can't put you in harm's way."

She stood her ground. "I insist. You can blindfold me, if you don't want me to know where I'm going, but I want to help you. Remember, it's also my country that's been brutalized."

Her determination was solid. After a short bout of verbal sparring, he relented with the proviso that she tuck her hair up under a cap and wear a loose fitting shirt with either jeans or slacks. "I can't risk anyone recognizing you, this is a dangerous game, Sister."

"I know, I know," she repeated. Thinking ahead, she decided to take the clothes with her to the dispensary where she did volunteer work two mornings a week. There was a utility room near the medicine cabinet where she could change after she got the syringes and epinephrine. She gave Jack the address and told him to meet her on the southwest corner of the street in front of the clinic.

He looked at the address and immediately opposed letting her walk alone in the dark. "You're not walking alone at this time of night." It was the same area where he'd sent Rio to buy drugs.

"I'll streak like a comet," the nun gestured wildly as she hurried around her living quarters gathering up her disguises.

"No matter, there'll be a tail on your comet. I'll be close by."

The pair left in sequence, first the stocky body of Sister Esther hurrying along with shopping bag in tow followed a few seconds later by a silhouette that floated in and out of the nocturnal voids. Fortunately, the dispensary was less than a half mile away and immediately on arrival Jack tucked himself into a pitch black space at the edge of a folding iron gate.

Sister Esther turned her key in the lock of the old medicine cabinet as she'd done many times before. Only this time she didn't sign the register, this time she crossed herself in good Catholic fashion and said quietly, "Please, forgive me." It was late and she knew there probably weren't more than three aides on duty, and as luck would have it, they were nowhere in sight. They had to have been attending to chores on the other end of the building and this allowed her to slip easily into the utility room to change clothes.

Her mission accomplished, the nun emerged from the building looking like a cross between a major league umpire and a postal employee. Even at this stage of the game, it brought a smile to the face of the seasoned agent. He edged into the streetlight and casually strolled alongside his undercover companion. "Good job," he complimented both her disguise and her enthusiasm. They walked briskly and vigilantly, Sister Esther carrying a rolled newspaper under her arm.

The entry behind the warehouse leading down to the cellar was pitch black. After the first few times of feeling his way up and down the stairway in the dark, Callahan could navigate the steps remarkably well. He took Sister Esther by the arm and guided her into a pernicious underworld where the air was rift with a mixture of raw earth and cigarette smoke. Coleman lanterns cast long greenish shadows in the manner of an El Greco painting.

Three guys sat at a table sifting intently through a mound of papers and barely acknowledged the entry of the two. Jack didn't bother with introductions. He directed the nun to a scruffy male subject who lay blindfolded, gagged, and shackled to a cot. The body on the cot was agitated, almost spastic as he tried to move. "He should be needing another fix about now, " Rio informed them as he bent down to survey his quarry.

Jack turned to the nun, "What we're gonna' do is give him just enough of his dope to keep him needing more. If he gets too comfortable on the fix, then you'll have to stimulate him a little, or maybe a lot, with your epinephrine. Hopefully, we'll be messing with his system enough to get him to talk. And... if you would, please, it would be better if you kept totally silent."

She acknowledged with a nod, and prepared herself mentally for the reprehensible task of looking at a human life as a disposable commodity. They went to work... .a collaborative effort of two new friends... in a repugnant situation trying to save their country of further victimization from this new age terrorism.

31

There he was… deposited right on the doorstep. Santa Fe arrived courtesy of a Ryder truck and in the company of two bewildered looking Gallery employees, who kept shaking their heads as if they had a twitch. Gage assumed this could rightly be called the Santa Fe twitch. All one could do after such a lengthy encounter with the artist would be to shake one's head to see if any kind of clarity would unscramble itself and fall compliantly into place. The next eight days would be extremely interesting, she concluded as she gave him a big hug.

He didn't respond to the hug, he was far more intrigued by the fact that Chicago had such a lengthy shore line. There was some little quirk of the mind that made him have to know right at that moment exactly how many miles. They were in the process of putting on a major show for the guy, and all he could talk about was the shore line. Gonna' be interesting was her only thought.

After she made arrangements with the gallery crew to unload the paintings, she made a move to get Santa Fe out of the way of the workers. He'd already tried to swap his Grateful Dead baseball cap for one of the workers Greenpeace cap. "Santa Fe, would you like to stay at my apartment until the show opens next weekend?" It didn't take much convincing, he always cried poor. She suspected he had considerable money tied up in securities, but to hear him talk he wasn't far from welfare. He joked about showing up at art openings and receptions for food and that was probably true, but it could also have something to do with keeping the obsessive compulsiveness tidiness of his apartment.

Bowing low and sweeping the ball cap across the horizon, he answered the question. "I'd be honored." Then with a quote from his beloved H.L. Mencken, he recounted, "Honor is simply the morality of superior men." He fidgeted a little. It was probably most uncomfortable for this extremely private man to have anyone in close proximity for an extended period of time, but on the other hand free lodging played to his frugal nature. He squirmed as if doing a dilemma dance, while his eyebrows scrunched into little squiggles. "Yep, I'd be honored." Frugal side won out.

Together they waited on retired Navy Captain, Jenk Wesley, more appropriately titled in this particular situation, neophyte Jenk Wesley. There was no way to prep anyone on Santa Fe, so next week would be a moment by moment event guaranteed to mess up the most logic of minds. Gonna' be fun, she told herself.

"Hey big guy," Gage called out as Jenk entered the office where she and the ponytailed artist were discussing the Ashcan school of painting. "Jenk Wesley, meet Santa Fe."

First a silent standoff, then a cautious handshake. "Howdy, pardner... you from Santa Fe?"

"I guess that's my name. How about you... you from Jenk?" Gage felt a smile starting to bubble up from deep down in her stomach. Oh yea, it was going to be a riot!

They started toward the gallery door with Santa Fe lugging an old duffel bag. Jenk offered to carry the beat-up gear and the artist readily accepted. The ride home wasn't exceptional, the artist was preoccupied with looking beyond the buildings for a shoreline. Jenk seemed amused but polite toward the newest occupant of the apartment, who spent the first evening entertaining them with off the wall dialogues. Not that he meant them to be off the wall, but, by ordinary human standards there was no other value to give them. Once Jenk and Gage found it was okay to laugh at his quirkiness, they enjoyed a week of one act comedies...a new one each night.

Santa Fe didn't have a problem with sleeping on the sofa. He slept on the floor in his studio. His bedtime rituals were idiosyncratic to say the least. From squeezing a tube of toothpaste to using a pair of nail clippers, he was fascinating to watch. It gave Gage further dimension in putting the exhibit together. But she also watched Jenk a lot during the next week. At times he'd disappear into the bedroom for long periods of time. At first, she thought maybe he'd reached artist overload, but then she'd hear him in lengthy phone conversations... conversations that were becoming more and frequent. In some ways, perhaps, his life was as quirky as Santa Fe's. He could go from a very serious phone demeanor straight to an outburst of enthusiasm for a card game.

Jenk found a formidable poker player under the zany facade of the painter. Santa Fe spent time in the Army, and as best they could glean from his explanation, the Army was for the sole purpose of teaching soldiers to play poker. As Jenk said gleefully, "Whatever the intent of the Army, thank you very much." They played for hours at night, also occasionally during the day when Gage didn't need Santa Fe at the gallery. The artist had an interesting story for each card, it took hours for a single game. Jenk didn't complain, at least he had someone to play with. It was the story about the three of clubs being a lily pad home for mama, papa, and baby frog that made Jenk choke on his beer. He swallowed a lot of laughs during that week of Army inspired poker.

The Missouri artist was actually quite competent to work with in the gallery setting. She tried to give him as much input into hanging the show as she could and he proved to have a flair. His introduction to the Board Members was memorable enough, jaws hanging open all around the conference table. He made a three minute speech that sounded like a eulogy to a Mexican jumping bean. Thankfully, they'd seen most of the paintings before the meeting and were very impressed with his work.

The ads and flyers were ready. Press blurbs were all out and there appeared to be considerable interest in the upcoming exhibit. Even the maven of make-or-break, Bery Paschal, gave a hearty thumbs up in her review. When Frank came to do the photo shoot, he'd already had an introduction to Santa Fe via the card games, but he was blown away by the clarity of color, to say nothing of the imagery fired onto the canvas by this capricious mind.

"Never seen anything like it," were Frank's exact words. He looked at her quizzically, "How are things going with the two roomates from opposite sides of the planet?"

Gage shrugged her shoulders, "Okay.... I just keep telling myself that all of this is temporary. Got time for a cup of coffee?"

"Time for you... always, but you're not supposed to go anywhere without your chaperone, are you?"

"I hate to tell him that he is as unnecessary as yesterday's newspaper. But he's so serious about watching over me," she confided as they walked toward the door.

They headed across the street to the coffee shop where each ordered the raspberry creme latte special. They sat down at the window where they could see the life size advertising posters of one of Santa Fe's acrylics. Impressive indeed, they both agreed. Gage finally spoke, "Are you going to be at the opening Friday evening?" But before she gave him time to answer she added, "Mr. Espinosa is so concerned with Santa Fe's unpredictability and persona that he told me this morning he wants to have a mock opening Thursday evening with the staff acting as patrons. Santa Fe's really not that unstable, but if the boss thinks we should, we will. His jumping bean spiel at the Board meeting was a tad over the top," she laughed. "You wanna' come. There won't be a card game Thursday night, cause whither I goest, he shall go too," she indicated lightheartedly.

"We'll see. I'm gonna' be there Friday evening for the opening, I'm not sure I wanna' do a pre- opening too."

She nodded an acceptance of his reasoning. "Are you seeing anybody, Frank?"

"Nope, including not seeing you either, since the new guys on the block have taken over," he let her know. "Come on I've got to get you back before Mr. Macho finds you missing."

"Frank, he's a nice guy. You even said so."

"I know," he grinned, "he's okay. I chafe a little at having to share your attention, that's all."

Gage weighed his response as they walked back across the street. Frank never said anything really personal to her about their relationship unless there was an obstacle, a safety net so to speak, to keep him from having to validate his remarks. She smiled. Men.... she thought to herself. They're so easy to read, so predictable.

"Thanks, friend," she kissed him on the cheek. "See you Friday, if not Thursday evening."

She went into her office to find Greta grabbing at a group of papers on her desk and Mr. Espinosa directing the whole process. What the hell, she puzzled. She was becoming defensive on Santa Fe's behalf because her boss was taking on shades of paranoia over this show.

She paused, "Can I do something?"

Mr. Espinosa hurriedly assured her they were going over the complicated chronology one more time, so he could feel confident interpreting the exhibit for their guests. That was bizarre, he was never less than confident about anything. She was beginning to think that maybe he just didn't like the exhibit.

As soon as he was out of sight, she pumped Greta for information. "What the heck was that all about? He never mingles with the guests that much anyway."

"Beats me, but he's sure got a burr up his butt," sighed Greta in graphic description. She thumbed through the notes Mr. Espinosa left with her and decided to put them in her purse for safekeeping. "Don't want to chance not following his orders properly." she explained to Gage, "I'll look at them again at home."

It was so routine at quitting time to hear Jenk's voice that Greta couldn't imagine otherwise now. "Hey girls... Gret, want to join us tonight for shrimp paella. I've got good fresh saffron for it."

"Sorry pal, I've got kids, remember?"

"No, not tonight, I lined up your sitter, bought Big Macs and rented a movie for them. I can see you gals gettin' uptight the closer this exhibit gets, so tonight we're relaxing."

"Are you for real? Gage, help me! Is this guy really standing here telling me that he got a sitter, fed my kids, and rented a movie," she all but gasped for air. "Don't wake me, I'm savoring this dream. Oh…what movie did you get?"

"Redford's *The Natural*, hope they haven't seen it."

"Perfect."

"Excuse me, if Mr. and Mrs. Mom and Pop are through taking care of the kids, let's go get the paella show on the road," Gage prompted. She wished something could work out between Greta and Jenk, but he mostly talked about the kids, and Gage didn't think Greta would ever dare to presume that this worldly hunk would be interested in her.

Santa Fe was waiting and became transfixed on the thought of paella. He tried to help, but kept them more entertained than doing anything productive toward insuring a meal. He did make one startling revelation. "Thursday evening, before my pre-opening opening, I want to take all of you to dinner. A good dinner, maybe my friend here," he turned his head toward Jenk, "will be so kind as to help me pick out a 'chow down' with a waterin' hole."

Jenk nodded, then erupted with a decent rendition of a Bob Dylan's, "The Times They Are A Changin". Gage thumped her ears as if to hear more clearly and all three soundly thanked Santa Fe for the invitation.

32

Thursday morning was a perfect weather day, an early November football looking day… a day of pom pon chrysanthemums backed with a solid team spirit. The only glitch in the ambience was the unsettled Mr. Espinosa and the flustered Greta. Santa Fe was rock solid steady. The show had to be a success. It was quality, it was unique, and it was going to be a crowd pleaser. It would provide a welcome respite from the sorrow of the New York disasters.

The artist promised to change his shoes… not his clothes, but his shoes… different shoes for each of the two opening nights. For Thursday night's pre-opening, he would wear red sneakers with the tux which he so gleefully advertised that he'd bought at Goodwill. But for the big Friday night opening, he'd change to Jesus sandals, as he called them.

The day went rapidly. The press was allowed access to the gallery all afternoon. Frank dropped by and Gage heard him ask Greta if everything was on track. It was really beginning to bug her that they weren't allowing Santa Fe a chance to prove himself. She had faith in the little guy and was looking forward to the evening for justification of her faith.

Jenk was an hour early to pick up his charges. Santa Fe strolled alongside him in his tux and red shoes… ready to take them out. They had to be back for the pre-opening at seven thirty, so they'd opted to get an early start on dinner. Jenk chose the restaurant well, great steaks cooked to the artist's supreme satisfaction. Santa Fe couldn't stop thanking him and finally Jenk pleaded with him to cease and desist in his gratitude. Gage felt that Jenk probably never believed that Santa Fe would actually follow through with paying the bill, until the artist finally pulled out his wallet and placed the money on the tray in front of him. Of course, he had to rearrange and realign the paper money over and over until Greta finally moved the tray away and called for the waiter to rescue it.

"Do I have time to stop by my place to freshen up a little," Gage asked Jenk?

"I think we can work it in," he replied nonchalantly.

Greta was once again impressed at the pilot's accommodating demeanor. "Amazing." She continued to repeat, "amazing," at intervals along the drive to the apartment. "Hey, honey, you might as well take your time and really doll up some, since our chauffeur is willing to wait," she snapped her fingers pretentiously. She caught a look in Jenk's eye and decided to tone it down a bit.

They waited while Gage hurried into a satin teddy with a black lace pullover and slender black skirt. The interim was long enough that it gave red sneakers enough time to take on the city of Chicago in a diatribe about Mrs. O'Leary's cow, which he kept getting confused with Timothy Leary, the guru of psychedelic drugs.

"You look perfect," Greta beamed on seeing her friend. "I look a mess."

"No you don't, but ask Jenk if we can run by your place, if you'd... " Before she could finish the sentence, he spoke up rather curtly to nix the idea.

"Okay, okay," she said soothingly, "we've all been a little testy today, let's go enjoy Mr. Espinosa's little soiree. But to herself she mumbled, "you've all been mucho testy today."

Even Nelson was working overtime. He delivered his usual movie trivia question as they scooted through the big brass doors. Santa Fe, of all people, stopped to try to figure out the answer to the doorman's query. "Come on," Gage finally called out to him.

Mr. Espinosa was standing, almost blocking the door to the main galleries as he steered them to a side room and indicated that before they had the pre-opening, he wanted to show a brief video while he had the staff together. "You come along too," he directed Santa Fe as he herded the other three toward the mahogany doors. As they entered the room, the normally taciturn Executive Director smiled at Gage, squeezed her hand and gave her a hug. Then with a wide gesture of his arm he acknowledged, "definitely the most meaningful show we've ever had."

Puzzled at the extrovert nature of Mr. Espinosa coupled with Santa Fe's gentle shoving motions, her bewilderment followed the line of dimmed lights along the room. A small orchestra was playing and people were casually milling about. In the faint glow of this side gallery, she saw her co-workers and her friends, including Frank, and Mr. and Mrs. Giovanni.

Her eye caught a single spotlight focused on a solitary work of art in the center of the room. And for the Metropolitan Special Exhibits Director, it was a monumental heart stopping moment. The vibrant, wistful painting on the easel was of one Gage Bayswater McClendon. She walked forward, not feeling the floor beneath her feet, and reached out slowly... touching the likeness, the incredible mirror likeness that looked back at her from the canvas. Her head was spinning, the voices fused into a transcendent chorus and the orchestra music resonated to the center of her soul. She stood alone, transfixed and unresponsive for a moment... unable to think... afraid to hope. An isolated tear trickled down her cheek, and a gentle hand reached out to wipe it away. Jack Callahan took her in his arms and brought the world back together again. The escalating strains of Ravel's Bolero once again played into their lives, this time in a salacious live orchestral crescendo. The handsome dragon man took a tiny gift from his pocket and pinned it on the blouse of the woman he adored. She looked down and smiled. They stood together, unmoving... locked in each other's eyes while the guests voiced approval and encouragement in provocative rhythmic hand clapping to the beguiling boil of the Spanish music.

Jenk swallowed hard, he knew he'd lost a partner. Across the room he could see the tiny golden rose that glistened on the black background of the lace blouse. Gage McClendon was, without a doubt, Jack Callahan's absolute achievement, the ultimate quest... his golden rose.

The music intensified. Existence outside their embrace faded... .and the Laramie man and the Chicago woman began to dance... .

VIGNETTES

Frank Beccaccio remained single, never again coming close to the type of friendship that he shared with Gage McClendon. He went on to win an international photo journalism award for a pictorial story on the outposts of post traumatic stress syndrome.

After sharing three wonderful years, Curtiss Markham-Raven Tall Wing died suddenly of an undiagnosed heart defect. Pliny stayed on the ranch maintaining the stoicism of her ancestors.

Sister Esther Concetta is still based in Singapore, but visits with Jack and Gage each time she comes back to the States. She and Jack Callahan have a very deep bond, no doubt relative to the al-Qaeda connection.

Mr. Giovanni became severely handicapped from a stroke, and Mrs. Giovanni brought in a 'boy toy' to cheer her up and take care of the household.

Navy Captain Jenk Wesley and Greta eventually became a couple. Greta joked that it was the only way he could stay close to his buddy. Jenk adapted easily to married life and reveled in caring for Greta's sons.

The Chicago show was an avenue of success for Santa Fe's quixotic philosophy and unique talent.

Jack and Gage McClendon Callahan were married soon after the 'one painting' gallery show. Gage stayed with Metropolitan Gallery. Jack retired the second time from the CIA and together with his buddy, Jenk Wesley, does consulting work for the Dept. of Defense. The Callahan couple is firmly convinced that theirs is the 'last great love story'.